CW00520091

Call of a Highlander

Katy Baker

Published by Katy Baker, 2019.

CALL OF A HIGHLANDER

First edition. January 12, 2019.

Chapter 1

The coffee shop was busy this morning. As Bethany Carter worked feverishly at the coffee machine, making the usual latte for Mr Penrose, she wiped her sweaty brow with a handkerchief and drew a deep breath. What else did she expect for a Monday morning in rainy Edinburgh? Everyone was eager for their morning pick-me-up before the start of a long working week and Beth didn't blame them. She could do with one herself.

Beth poured the drink into a tall glass before placing it on a tray and pushing it across the counter to Mr Penrose.

"There you go," she said, smiling. "A bit of energy before your meeting. Today's the day, isn't it?"

Mr Penrose grinned. In his sixties, he had a booming laugh that belied his slight frame, and a fringe of white hair around his head. He'd been coming into the coffee shop for as long as Beth had been working there.

"It certainly is, lassie!" he said. "Those idiots in HR willnae know what's hit them when I present my counter-proposal!"

Beth laughed. "I don't doubt it. Good luck, Mr Penrose."

"Ye have my thanks, lass. Without yer sage advice I never would have gotten this far."

"Oh, I only pointed you in the right direction. And you did see a proper lawyer like we discussed?"

Mr Penrose was at logger-heads with his employers who were trying to get rid of him as he was getting on a bit and was a little slower than he used to be. When he'd mentioned this to Beth, she'd been outraged and been unable to stop herself giving him some free legal advice. She couldn't just stand by and see Mr Penrose bullied by a big corporation could she? And besides, what else was she supposed to do with her law degree? But she'd insisted he see a registered lawyer as well.

Mr Penrose nodded. "Of course. I'll pop in tomorrow and let ye know how it went." He wrapped his hands around his coffee cup and swept out.

The line was getting longer and Beth, along with her three colleagues, were kept busy for a good hour serving cappuccinos and lattes, Americanos and espressos, until finally there was a lull and Beth leaned back on the counter to take a breather. She glanced at the clock on the wall and a thrill of trepidation ran through her. It was 9.00 am.

"Mind if I take a quick break?" she said to Callie, her supervisor.

Callie, a petite blonde with her hair tied back in a plait, looked up from where she was wiping down the counter. She glanced at her watch and then at Beth with a look of sympathy on her face.

"Nine o'clock on the dot as always. If they hadn't responded by close of play last night, I doubt they would have this early. Maybe wait a while?"

Beth shook her head, nerves wriggling in her belly. It was all she could do not to bite her nails. "I can't. The wait is killing me! It's been three weeks already. They said I'd hear in two." She hated the desperation in her voice but couldn't control it. She *was* getting desperate. This application was practically her last chance. If they didn't accept her...

"Sure," Callie said with a smile. "And, honey? Good luck."

Beth smiled at her friend then hurried into the office. Seating herself in the swivel chair, she turned on the PC and logged in. Her stomach did somersaults as she waited for her email to load. Chewing her thumbnail, she scanned her inbox and her heart skipped a beat as she saw a message from MacArthur and Sons Solicitors sitting there.

Oh god! This was it! With trembling fingers she clicked on the email and opened it, the nerves turning to excitement. They'd finally replied! They *would* accept her! They would!

But as her eyes scanned the email, the excitement turned to ashes. *We regret to inform you that after careful consideration we are unable to offer you an internship at MacArthur and Sons. We wish you the very best in your future endeavors.*

Beth read the words again. And then a third time, willing them to change, to become the words she'd been longing to hear. But they didn't. She leaned back in the chair, staring at the screen and the ruin of her dreams.

It was over. MacArthur and Sons had been her last hope of an internship. Having come to Edinburgh from the US four years ago on a student visa and then graduating with a degree in Law and Criminology, Beth needed to find an internship with a company willing to sponsor her working visa if she was ever to fulfil her dream of becoming a human rights lawyer. If she didn't find such an internship her student visa would expire in a month's time and she'd have no choice but to leave the city that had become her home, the city that had offered her the shelter and the fresh start she'd so badly needed.

Beth felt tears gathering in her eyes and dashed them away mercilessly. No. She would not give in! There were at least two other firms she'd yet to try. She wasn't beaten yet! She *would* become a human rights lawyer if it was the last thing she ever did, dammit!

She logged out, pushed to her feet, and straightened her hair and uniform before making her way into the shop. Callie looked up with a question in her eyes but Beth ignored her friend's enquiry. She couldn't face it yet. Instead, she grabbed a cloth and went about wiping down tables and gathering up dirty cups and plates.

What had she done wrong? The interview had gone well and they'd seemed impressed by her academic record. Damn it, damn it, damn it! What the hell would she do now?

She was so preoccupied that she took no notice of the occupant at the table she was wiping until a voice said, "My, ye will wear a hole in that if ye aren't careful, lass."

Beth blinked and looked up to see an old woman seated at the table. She seemed incredibly old, with iron gray hair pulled back in a bun and a nest of wrinkles around her eyes and mouth. Her age-spotted hands were clasped on the table in front of her but the gaze she fixed on Beth burned with a fierce intelligence.

"Oh! Sorry," Beth said. "I was miles away."

"Aye, I can see that," the woman replied. "Ye look as though ye have the weight of the world on yer shoulders."

The woman's gaze was piercing and her eyes, Beth noticed, were so dark as to be almost black. The iris and pupil melded into one, making them seem like chips of obsidian. Beth shifted, suddenly uncomfortable.

"I...um...you haven't got a drink. Can I get you a coffee?"

The woman waved a dismissive hand. "Coffee? Foul stuff for heathens! I'll have a cup of yer finest tea, my dear, and perhaps a slice of cake to go with it."

Beth smiled. "Tea and cake it is. Coming right up."

She returned a moment later carrying a tray loaded with a teapot and a slice of Victoria Sponge—her favorite. She placed it on the table before the old woman.

"Enjoy."

The old woman smiled up at her. "I'm sure I will, lass. I reckon it's just what I need."

She stared up at Beth, unblinking. The old woman's gaze seemed to pierce her to the bone and a sudden shiver of unease walked down Beth's spine. The old woman suddenly held out a hand.

"I'm Irene, my dear. Irene MacAskill."

"Oh. Nice to meet you. I'm Beth. Bethany Carter." She reached out and shook the old woman's hand.

As her fingers touched the warm, papery skin, Beth suddenly staggered. Dizziness washed through her and for a second her vision wavered. The coffee shop disappeared and she saw mist-wreathed mountains and sparkling lochs. A man was walking towards her. She couldn't see his face but she knew him, knew him better than she knew herself...

Her vision cleared and she was suddenly back in the coffee shop again. She steadied herself on the back of a chair.

"I'm...I'm...sorry," she muttered. "I don't know what came over me."

Irene MacAskill patted her hand gently. "It takes some people like that sometimes, my dear."

Beth looked at her quizzically. "What does?"

"Destiny. It can be a wrench when ye confront it for the first time. As ye just did. But it canna be avoided, whether we wish it or no. Yers is coming for ye, Bethany Carter. It will soon find ye and then ye will have a choice to make. Will ye confront it? Or will ye run?"

The back of Bethany's neck prickled. She pulled her hand from Irene's grasp. "What are you talking about?"

"Oh, I think ye know," the old woman replied. "Ye are running, my dear. Running from the past, thinking that if ye can only become a lawyer ye can somehow fix the wrongs that were done to ye. But it doesnae work that way. Ye canna find happiness by running from yer past: only by running towards yer future. Are ye ready to do that, Bethany Carter? Are ye ready to find yer true path?"

Those dark eyes of hers seemed to bore into Beth's soul. A little freaked out now, she took a step back.

"Who are you? What do you want with me?"

Irene smiled, a kindly expression creasing her face. "Only what ye want for yerself, lass. For ye to find yer place in the world and in so doing, help me to save a life. A precious life although many wouldnae think so. If that life is snuffed out, the balance will be thrown out of kilter. Only ye can do what needs to be done."

"Me?" Beth said with a snort. "I think you've got the wrong person."

"Have I? Are ye sure about that? Dinna ye want to right the wrongs of the world? Isnae that why ye are so set on becoming a lawyer?"

"I...um...yes," Beth stammered. How the hell did this woman know so much about her? She was officially creeped out. "Look. I have to get back to work. Enjoy the tea."

She began to walk off but Irene's hand shot out and gripped her hand. The woman's fingers were as cold and hard as iron. After a moment she released her grip and Beth realized she'd deposited a piece of paper in Beth's hand.

"What's this?"

Irene smiled. "That is for ye to find out—if ye so choose. If ye truly wish to right a wrong and mayhap find yer true path into the bargain, ye may wish to take a look."

Irene MacAskill climbed to her feet. She was so short the top of her head barely reached Beth's shoulder. The old woman squeezed Beth's arm. "Until we meet again, my dear."

Without another word, Irene walked to the door, her tea and cake untouched on the table. Beth stared after her long after she'd disappeared.

"You okay?" Callie asked as Beth shuffled behind the counter. "You look a little pale."

"I'm fine," Beth replied. "Just a little tired."

She stuffed the piece of paper Irene had given her into a pocket and busied herself making a couple of espressos for two businessmen in sharp suits. After that it was a cappuccino and latte for a young couple then a mocha for a guy in running gear. She tried to lose herself in the monotony of the work but Irene's words had unsettled her. Who was she? And why had she said those things? How was Beth suppose to right a wrong she didn't even know about? The incident had left her feeling edgy and unsettled, particularly coming so quickly after her rejection by MacArthur and Sons.

She placed two drinks on a tray and pushed it across the counter towards a middle-aged couple standing there.

The woman frowned. "Sorry, I asked for two espressos."

Beth startled. "You did? Oh, of course you did. Sorry. One moment."

She wiped at her forehead and began making the espressos. Damn it! She couldn't seem to concentrate at all. *Get a grip!* she told herself fiercely. The last thing she needed was to make a mess of this job. Then where would she be?

But as she went to put the espressos onto the tray her hands suddenly slipped. The tray tipped and the cups went crashing to the floor with the splinter of breaking crockery, splashing hot coffee over the floor and the bottom of Beth's pants.

"Oh! Sorry!" Beth cried. She knelt to clear it up but Callie stepped smoothly in front of her.

"I'll sort it. Why don't you take a minute?"

Beth looked into the concerned eyes of her friend and sagged. She suddenly felt exhausted. "Okay. Thanks."

Leaving the couple in Callie's capable hands, Beth all but fled into the back room and perched on the desk. Rubbing her eyes with the heels of her hands, she tried to calm her thumping heart. Today was not going well. Maybe she should rewind and not bother getting out of bed this morning. That way perhaps she'd still have some hope of a future. Maybe that way she'd not feel so wrung out and wretched as she did right now.

You're just stressed, she told herself. *You need rest.*

Do I? she thought. *Or do I need something else entirely?*

She paused suddenly. Irene MacAskill's words played in her head. *Right a wrong. Find yer true path.* Beth couldn't seem to get them out of her mind. On impulse she pulled the bit of paper Irene had given her from her pocket and smoothed it out. It was a flyer for a guest house a few miles outside the city. She frowned at it. Why had Irene given her this?

The guesthouse looked quaint and comfortable and a million miles away from Beth's problems. She was suddenly caught with a longing to see the place. Irene might be a crazy old crackpot but she'd made Beth realize one thing: she needed a break.

Callie opened the door, crossed to the desk and perched next to Beth.

"You want to talk about it?"

Beth sighed. "Sorry about just now. I shouldn't have got that order wrong or dropped the coffee."

"Stuff the coffee! I'm talking about you! You've been out of sorts since you went to check your email. What's wrong?"

Beth took a deep breath and looked at her friend. "I heard back. They rejected me."

"Ah, shit. I'm sorry. But you'll find another company, right?"

"Sure," Beth lied. "There are loads of law firms I haven't tried yet."

"And until one of them snaps you up we've got plenty of shifts here to keep you going. I swear we get busier by the day. The people of Edinburgh must have their coffee!"

"Actually, I was hoping for some time off," Beth said holding up the flyer. "Do you fancy it? This weekend? We could have a girly weekend away!"

Callie shook her head. "Sounds fab but I can't. I'm on rota all weekend and I think Adrian will kill me if I ask to change shift again—you know how he gets."

"Okay," Beth said, waving a hand. "Never mind. It was only an idea."

"You should go though," Callie said. "You've earned it. When was the last time you had some time off? Ever?"

Beth thought about it. She'd been on a few trips during her various training placements but that had been for study rather than leisure. "You're right. I am going to go. A few days of breakfast in bed and wandering round tourist sites will do me good."

Callie grinned. "That's more like it. Now let's get out there. If Mrs Monroe doesn't get her frappe and croissant soon I reckon she'll scream the place down."

Beth nodded, her expression mock-serious. "Ah, it's an emergency then. Come on!"

Chapter 2

Camdan MacAuley's lungs burned with exertion and the muscles in his thighs and calves ached with weariness but he didn't stop. He had no idea how long he'd been running, hours maybe. Around him the autumn woodland showed its splendor in a riot of red and gold under an unseasonably blue sky. Cam barely noticed. His booted feet kicked up clods of sodden leaves and left footprints in the soft earth of the Highland soil. He ran rhythmically, mechanically, his long stride eating up the miles, the clear air and physical exertion gradually settling his thoughts in a way few things could these days.

Cam jumped a stream, came down easily on the other side, and then powered up the rise beyond without breaking stride. He sprinted to the top of the hill, sending a flock of grouse winging into the air, then skidded to a halt and looked down on the scene below.

In the distance he could see smoke rising from the settlement of Cannoch. Sitting at the convergence of two major rivers, it was a prosperous settlement and had been Cam's home for the last month—the longest he'd stayed in one place for a long time. He'd taken employment as a merchant's guard: steady, easy work with decent pay and the promise of a warm bed. Much better than what Cam was used to these days.

He shielded his eyes from the sun and gazed out over the settlement, feeling an unexpected pang of longing. It had been good to feel grounded again. To stay in one place more than a few days and to begin to get to know it and its people. It was the nearest he would ever get to the clan life he'd lost, even if it was only for a few weeks.

Listen to ye, he thought. *Carping on like some old woman! Ye chose exile, remember? And ye did it willingly. It's nay good crying over what's done. There's nay going back.*

Yesterday the merchant he'd worked for had packed up and moved south, eager to reach the lowlands before winter closed the passes, and so Camdan had taken his pay, collected his gear from the lodging house, and left. He'd spent last night camped in the woods alone. It was just as well. He'd tarried too long in Cannoch. He could feel his rage beginning to take hold, that simmering fury that could only be soothed by violence. He'd held it in check whilst in the village, succumbing only to a couple of tavern fights that were more bluster than anything serious, but now he could feel it starting to bite. It was one of the reasons he'd gone running this morning.

With a last look down at Cannoch, Camdan turned away, sprinted down the hill and into the untamed countryside to the north. An hour or so later he reached his camp. His horse, Firefly, was cropping grass nearby. War-trained and temperamental, the gelding was the only thing Cam kept from his former life. If anyone wondered why a simple mercenary rode a war horse fit for the nobility, they didn't comment. Perhaps they assumed the horse was the spoils of war.

He whistled and Firefly came trotting over, sniffing his master's hand and snorting in greeting.

"Did ye miss me, boy?" Cam asked, scratching the horse behind the ears. "Stand."

The horse obeyed, waiting patiently whilst Cam examined his hooves, checking the shoes were still snugly fitted. He would not risk laming Firefly through carelessness. Cam's father, Laird David MacAuley, had impressed the importance of looking after one's mount onto all three of his sons. In battle a warrior's mount could mean the difference between life and death. It was a lesson Cam had never forgotten.

Satisfied with his inspection, he gave Firefly a measure of oats from the saddlebag then seated himself on a log. The sweat on his body was starting to dry and the autumn air held a chill so he toweled himself dry and pulled on his spare shirt, tying the sash of his MacAuley plaid over his chest.

When this was done he ate a quick breakfast of dried meat and yesterday's bread then packed away his camp and saddled Firefly. Taking the reins, he led the big horse across the clearing, heading north. It seemed as good a direction as any.

His thoughts were elsewhere, his mind preoccupied, so he jumped when a figure suddenly stepped out into the sunlit glade in front of him. Startled from his thoughts, Cam reacted instinctively. He drew his sword in one quick sweep. The blade glittered in the sunlight as the point came to rest against the throat of the newcomer. The sudden danger sent the rage coursing through his veins like molten metal. His arm quivered with the effort of restraining himself from driving his blade through the newcomer's throat.

"Ye have nay need of that," said a voice. "I am not yer enemy, nor have I come to cause ye harm."

Only then did Cam realize that it wasn't some bandit or footpad come to rob him that stood before him. It was an old woman. She was tiny, barely reaching Cam's chest, and seemed old beyond years. Her weathered skin was creased like old parchment and dark eyes stared out at him, unflinching and unafraid.

Sudden shame washed through him. Was this what he'd become? The mighty Camdan MacAuley, greatest warrior of the MacAuley clan, reduced to threatening defenseless old women? He stepped back, sheathed his sword, then put his arm across his chest and gave the old woman a bow of which any courtier would have been proud.

"My...my... apologies," he stammered. "I was startled. I meant no offense."

"And none has been taken, my lad," the old woman said, her joviality belying the fact she'd had a sword blade pressed against her throat only a moment before.

Camdan frowned. Why was an old woman roving the woods alone? Where were her kin?

"Are ye lost?" he asked carefully. "If ye wish, I will escort ye back to Cannoch. This isnae a place to be wandering alone."

"Isnae it?" she asked. "Then why are *ye* out here?"

"I...I....I'm a traveler," he replied, not liking the way her gaze bored into him.

"Oh? And where are ye traveling to, Camdan MacAuley?"

He took a step back, suddenly startled. "How do ye know who I am?"

She smiled. "Who else would ye be? Who else wanders the wilds wearing the MacAuley plaid? Who else but the cursed brother of Laird MacAuley?"

A shiver walked down Cam's spine. "What are ye talking about, woman?" he snapped, his heart suddenly thumping. "I dinna know what ye speak of."

The woman stepped so close she had to crane her head back to look up at him. She was a little over half his height and easily three times his age, but in that moment, her presence seemed to fill the clearing like a thundercloud. "I think ye do, my boy. I think ye know exactly of what I speak. So I ask again: where are ye going, Camdan MacAuley?"

Who was this stranger to question him so? Anger made his tone sharp. "Who are ye? What do ye want with me?"

"My name is Irene MacAskill ," she replied. "And as for what I want with ye, only what ye want for yerself. Peace. For ye and for the balance. Ye have wandered far, far from the paths of yer destiny."

"Destiny?" he said bitterly. "I once believed in such a thing. That was a long time ago and I've since learned the error of my ways. There isnae any such thing as destiny. There is only duty. And then death."

Her gaze softened and something like sympathy crossed her face. "Oh, my boy. What has been done to ye?"

Her words stung him to anger. "I neither need nor want yer pity, woman! Now step aside!"

She seemed not in the least daunted by his tone. "It isnae pity I've come to offer ye, Camdan MacAuley, but redemption."

Cam froze. Redemption? For him? After all he'd done? "What do ye mean?"

"Ye made a choice all those years ago, ye and yer brothers," Irene said. "Ye believe that choice has condemned ye. But there are always other choices, other paths to tread. It isnae too late if ye have the courage to face yer past and change the course of yer future."

"Bah! Ye speak in riddles, woman!" Cam growled. "I dinna have time for such nonsense."

He grabbed Firefly's reins and moved to walk past her but the old woman clasped his wrist with fingers as strong as tree roots.

"Yer choice is coming, Camdan. When it does ye will need all yer courage if ye are to do what needs to be done, if ye are to break yer curse and find a new path to walk, one that leads away from violence and loneliness and back into the light. It is a path that ye canna walk alone. Ye will need to open yer heart. Can ye do that, Camdan MacAuley?"

Cam opened his mouth for an angry retort but the words died in his throat. The expression on her face stilled him. There was a deep sorrow in her eyes, one that seemed to span the ages. His anger drained away.

"I canna," he whispered at last. "I dinna know how."

She let go of his wrist and nodded sadly. "Then ye must learn. If ye dinna then the future of yer clan is lost."

With that she walked away. Cam watched her go, perplexed.

"Wait!" he called after a moment, hurrying after her. "Ye canna just go wandering the woods by yerself! I will take ye back to—"

His words stuttered to a halt as he realized the trail ahead was empty. Spinning around, he scanned the area but detected nothing except the quiet, sunlit woods. Kneeling, he searched the ground for footprints. The soft, damp earth should have shown signs of her passage but there were none.

Camdan straightened, a sudden foreboding tightening his stomach. No old woman could disappear so quickly. And how did she know who he was? How did she know of his bargain?

Fae, a voice whispered in his mind like a warning. He felt suddenly cold, despite the sunlight falling on his skin. He'd hoped the Fae were done with him. It seemed he was wrong.

Crossing to Firefly, he pulled his cloak from the saddlebag, swung it around his shoulders, and then climbed into the saddle. He set his heels to the horse's flanks and fled.

Chapter 3

The sat nav on Beth's dashboard beeped, telling her to take the next left. She obeyed, passing a sign that read *Welcome to Banchary* in English, with the Gaelic equivalent scrawled underneath. It was a small village that boasted a pub and a post office and lay a few miles outside Edinburgh.

Following the directions on the flyer Irene MacAskill had given her, she drove through the village and pulled up at the *Castle View Guesthouse*, a large and pretty building that looked Georgian. Turning off the engine, she grabbed her bag and stepped out of the car.

The rain that had fallen incessantly during her drive from the city had finally cleared, leaving a sparkling, fresh afternoon. Beth looked around and sucked in a deep breath of the clean, still air. It settled into her lungs and as she breathed out some of her tension went with it. Yes, this had been a good idea. The stillness of the rural afternoon was a million miles away from the bustling busyness of Edinburgh. It was just what she needed.

Hefting her bag, she made her way into the reception area where she was met by a stout woman by the name of Veronica Hughes, the owner of the guesthouse. She smiled warmly at Beth.

"Ah! Our American guest! Very pleased to meet ye, my dear. I trust yer drive out from the capital wasnae too bad?"

"Not too bad," Beth agreed. "It's not far once you get clear of the city traffic. It was just a bit wet."

Veronica snorted at that. "Aye, well ye get used to it. Still, I reckon we are in for a grand evening. Once the rain has blown through, it makes the hills and loch seem to sparkle in the sunshine. Now, let me show ye up to yer room."

Beth followed the woman up a set of winding stairs to the first floor where she was escorted to a sumptuous room that was far too big for one person. The king-size bed alone was enough to drown her and on seeing it Beth suddenly wanted nothing more than a long soak in the bath and then to curl up on that bed with a good book.

Mrs Hughes busied herself about the room, straightening bed covers that didn't need straightening and making sure the towels in the bathroom were arranged perfectly, chattering all the while about the sights Beth might want to visit whilst she was here.

Beth smiled at the woman's friendly chatter. She wandered to the window and looked out. Her room was at the rear of the building and through the window she had an unspoilt view of the undulating landscape reaching all the way to the horizon. She drew a sharp breath. No wonder Irene had said this was a place to relax. Golden and red woodlands cloaked the hills and the twinkle of a loch glittered under the late afternoon sun. This place might be close to Edinburgh but it felt like another world.

Bringing her gaze closer to home, she spotted something in the field behind the guesthouse. The moss-covered ruins of a building rose out of the ground. She couldn't tell what it had once been but half-tumbled walls and window casings overgrown with ivy poked from the ground like bones. Despite the afternoon sunlight, the structure remained dark and forbidding as though it resisted the sun's attempt to illuminate it.

"I've left some extra soap in the dispenser and there are more blankets in the wardrobe if ye'd like them. Just ring down if ye need anything else," Mrs Hughes said.

"Thanks." Beth pointed at the ruins. "What is that place?"

"Ah, so ye've spotted our local attraction. It's called Fingal's castle and it's where Castle View guesthouse gets its name. It isnae a castle really. Nobody really knows what it used to be although it's very, very old. Legends around here say it was once a dwelling place of the Fae. The stories say never to visit on the dark of the moon or the solstices because that's when the Fae gather there to dance. They dinna suffer mortals to see such things and will spirit ye away to their world." She laughed. "Although I canna say we've lost too many tourists that way!" She patted Beth on the shoulder. "It's just an old ruined croft but dinna tell my husband I said that. He reckons these old tales keep the tourists coming in."

Beth smiled. "Your secret is safe with me."

"I'll leave ye to it then. Give me a shout if ye need anything."

She left Beth alone in the room. Beth stared out of the window. Despite Mrs Hughes' reassurances, the sight of the ruins made her vaguely uncomfortable. She couldn't quite determine why.

It's Irene MacAskill's talk of destiny and Mrs Hughes going on about the Fae and all that crap, she told herself. *It's got me on edge. Those things are just stones, that's all. And Irene MacAskill is just some crazy old woman. And maybe I'm a little crazy for taking her advice and coming here in the first place.*

"I should have booked a spa weekend," she muttered to herself. "What was I thinking?"

With a snort of exasperation, Beth turned away from the window, made her way down the stairs and out of the back of the building. The breeze plucked at her clothing, bringing with it the scent of earth and pine needles. Ahead stretched the guesthouse lawn and beyond this was a gate that let out into the field beyond. Beth let herself through the gate. The ruins of Fingal's Castle lay directly ahead of her. From down here they seemed bigger, more imposing than they had from the bedroom window.

Just stones, she told herself. *A bunch of moldy old ruins.*

An information board had been placed a few meters away. On it were some artist's renderings of dancing fairies and the story of Fingal's Castle—the same story that Mrs Hughes had told her. It looked like something right out of a kid's fairy tale. Yes, this place was definitely a tacky tourist trap.

She examined the ruins. The outer wall formed a broad rectangle with tumbled walls inside dividing the place into rooms. Snapping some images on her camera phone, Beth did a circuit of the site. This late in the afternoon the tourists had gone and she had the place to herself. In one corner of the site a staircase spiraled up against the wall, ending in mid-air with ivy hanging off the end. In another room she spied the remains of a fireplace big enough for her to stand in. Another room had a circular pit covered with an iron grate that she guessed was a well.

The whole place was eerily silent. Even her boots made no noise on the flagstones.

She completed a circuit and returned to where she'd started. Shielding her eyes against the bright afternoon sunlight, she squinted and saw an old archway looming above her. This might once have been the main entrance to the building but no door remained and the walls to either side were half-collapsed, leaving only the archway which yawned like a black, hungry mouth. A sign read: *Danger, keep out.*

She raised her cell phone to snap a picture, but paused as something odd caught her eye. The dark space beneath the archway looked strangely shimmery and as she watched, images began to form in the air, fuzzy, as though she was looking through frosted glass.

"What the—?" Beth muttered, stepping closer.

The images coalesced until she saw a ring of standing stones on a lonely shoreline. Three men stood inside. They were speaking but Beth couldn't hear the words. Two were dark-haired, the other strawberry blond. A small, wizened old man stood facing them. With a malicious grin, the old man stepped forward and suddenly the circle blazed with light, blinding her. It winked out and Beth saw another image. The blond man sitting alone by a campfire, surrounded by darkness. She couldn't make out his face.

"I'm going crazy" she murmured. She reached out as though to touch the images. "I'm seeing things now."

"Aye, lass," said a voice suddenly. "Ye are seeing things as they were, as they are, and as they may yet be—if the balance isnae restored."

Beth whirled to find Irene MacAskill standing behind her. The tiny woman wore a long coat that flapped in the breeze and wisps of gray hair had escaped her bun. She smiled warmly up at Beth.

"You!" Beth cried. "What are you doing here?"

"Where else would I be?"

Beth blinked. "You mean you live here? In Banchary?"

"All of Alba is my home, lass. Alba of then, of now, and of yet to come."

"Okaaay," Beth said, taking a slow step away. She had a feeling this conversation was going to go about as well as the one in Edinburgh had. *I need a stiff drink or five,* she thought. *I must be more stressed than I thought. I'm hallucinating and talking to crazy old women! Why the hell did I come here?*

But the images beneath the archway were still there. They looked pretty real to her. Too real in fact as though she looked through a window into some place...other.

"Aye," Irene said, moving up beside her. "It isnae easy to escape is it? Destiny, I mean. It pulls us whether we wish it or nay."

"What's happening?" Beth asked, a little frightened now. "What am I looking at?"

Irene rolled her eyes. "Dinna I keep telling ye? Yer destiny, lass.

"There's no such thing," Beth snapped. "Is this some sort of trick? Or a scam to catch unsuspecting tourists?" She couldn't hide the edge of anger in her voice. She was tired and had come up here to relax. Now she felt more confused and bewildered than ever.

A sad smile crossed Irene's face. "Ah, I'm sorry, lass. If I could spare ye this, I would. But it isnae my choice. I am but the keeper of the balance. I do what I must. As ye must."

Beth stared at the old woman for a long moment and then looked at the archway. The image had changed again and now all she could see were waves lapping against a lonely shore. "What do you mean? What must I do?"

Irene laid a hand on Beth's wrist. Her skin was warm and dry, like brittle leaves. "Ye must restore the balance. Right a great wrong, fix an injustice. If ye do, there is a chance ye will find yer own path and the thing ye seek most in the world."

"You don't know what I seek," Beth protested.

"Dinna I?" Irene said kindly. "I know what ye are running from, my dear. I know the pain that awaits ye if ye return to yer homeland and what caused it. I know the fear that hides deep in yer heart. It sits there like a worm in an apple and will consume ye if ye let it. Ye must confront it, my dear. Walk the path ye were meant to walk and mayhap ye will nay longer be afraid."

Her words pelted Beth like stones. She suddenly remembered that cold January night when there had been a knock on her door and everything had changed.

"No!" she said fiercely, shaking her head and pushing the memories away. "You're wrong and I won't listen to you!"

Irene squeezed her arm. Her dark eyes shone with compassion. "Yer choice is here, lass. What will ye do? If ye wish, ye can turn around, return to the guesthouse and continue with yer life. But there is a second choice. Ye can step under the archway. It will lead ye down a dark, dangerous path but one that, if ye have the courage to walk it, will also lead ye to the light. To yer destiny."

She looked up at the archway. It seemed to beckon her closer like a promise.

Turn around, a voice whispered a warning in her head. *Turn around and walk away. This is insane!*

But a deeper, more insistent voice whispered that this was right. It was where she was meant to be. Beth didn't understand it but found herself taking a step towards the archway. Then another. The images disappeared, to be replaced by a shimmering curtain, like heat-haze over a bonfire. Her skin tingled and a tugging sensation flared in her stomach, drawing her closer.

Taking a deep breath, Beth stepped through the arch.

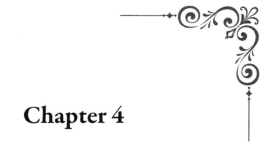

Chapter 4

As he rode Camdan tried to put the meeting with Irene MacAskill out of his mind. It was hard. The strange old woman's words had unsettled him, making the rage rear up inside. It burned through his veins, the bite of a hundred tiny flames. Anger surged beyond his ability to control it.

Sensing his master's mood, Firefly stamped and shied and Camdan reined him in savagely. From up ahead he heard the sound of shouting. Setting his heels to Firefly's flanks, he sent the horse charging forward.

He burst into a clearing where two foresters had been cornered by a band of ragged-looking ruffians. One of the foresters held a staff as he defended his comrade who had blood dripping down his temple. Facing them across the clearing were five men, all lean-looking and well armed. Camdan, with his soldier's training, assessed the scene in an instant. With a surge of fury he drove Firefly between the two groups, forcing the brigands back a pace.

"Go!" he bellowed at the foresters. "Flee!"

The one with the staff grabbed his comrade and they fled into the woods. Camdan turned to face the brigands. Their leader, a large man with a scar down his face, spat on the ground.

"Damn ye," he growled. "Ye will pay for that."

Cam jumped from his horse and slowly drew his sword. He grinned manically at the men as they fanned out around him, weapons drawn.

"I hoped ye'd say that."

Camdan waited patiently, the tip of his sword resting in the dirt. The five men circled him like a wolf-pack stalking its prey. Camdan didn't move. His senses tingled with awareness. He could hear every rustle of their clothing, smell their sweat, feel the soft pad of their feet on the ground. They thought they had him trapped. They thought five against one were good odds.

They were wrong.

The first man lunged in, a heavy thrust aiming at Cam's heart. Cam swiftly side-stepped then swung his own blade. The rage surged in his veins, the fury, the bloodlust he struggled to control, and he felt his lips pull back in a feral smile.

Cam brought his sword up, blocking the stroke and the two blades met with a squeal of metal. Cam's grin widened. The outlaws were better than expected. This would be a good fight.

BETH FELT A STRANGE sense of falling even though she could still feel the solid ground beneath her feet. For a second her vision went black and dizziness swamped her. She slumped to her knees and her hands came down on cold, wet earth. The smell of leaf litter filled her nostrils.

With an effort she climbed to her feet and looked around wildly. Ahead of her stretched an expanse of woodland, the leaves a sea of gold and red which swayed gently in the breeze. Where was the field? Where were the ruins of Fingal's Castle?

She turned. The archway reared behind her and jagged ruins poked through the leaf-covered ground. But they looked different to the ruins of Fingal's Castle and the landscape had totally changed. There was no sign of the guesthouse. Instead, trees marched into the distance for as far as she could see.

Beth pressed the heels of her hands against her forehead. "Shit," she murmured. "What the hell is going on?"

Her heart thumped in her chest and the beginnings of panic fluttered at the edges of her mind. She turned around, looking for Irene, but found no trace of the old woman.

"Irene!" she yelled. "Where are you?"

There was no response but the whistling of the wind through the branches and the faint echo of her call against the stones of the ruins. Taking a deep breath, Beth marched back through the archway, waiting for the sense of falling that she'd experienced before. It didn't come. Rather than stepping back into the field in Banchary, she found herself walking inside what might once have been the main hall of whatever this place had been. It had crumbling walls and no roof but even so, there was far more left of it than the ruins of Fingal's Castle in her time.

Beth froze. In her time? Where had that thought come from? She pushed it away. No. She would not follow that thought. There must be a logical explanation for this. There had to be. She just had to figure out what.

Wrapping her arms around herself, Beth turned around slowly, examining the hall. An old fireplace stood at one end and she saw that the stone was carved with a series of strange markings. A swirling pattern of interlocked coils covered it, and as she looked closer, Beth saw the same pattern repeated throughout the room, carved into the walls and even the floor. She shivered. There was something about that pattern that made her decidedly uneasy.

The shadows suddenly seemed ominous and Beth hurried back outside into the sunlight.

"Irene!" she bellowed with all her strength. "Where the hell are you? This is not funny!"

Her shout faded into silence, muffled by the thick foliage. Beth pressed a shaky hand to her forehead and forced herself to think.

My cell!

She fumbled in her coat pocket and pulled out the phone. She flicked it on and immediately dialed 999 for the emergency services. Right now the sight of the flashing blue lights of a police car would be the most welcome sight in the world. But the cell gave out a shrill beep that had her snatching it away from her ear. Examining the screen, she saw an icon flashing in the corner that indicated no signal.

Great! Absolutely fantastic!

Keep calm, she told herself. *Think. You need to figure out where you are and then find your way back to Banchary. This is Scotland. It won't be hard to find a road or a house or someone who can give you a lift.*

"Come on, Beth," she said. "You won't figure anything out just standing here."

She set off, making a circuit of the building, searching for an access road or a trail that might lead to a bigger thoroughfare. She found nothing. The site seemed to be completely surrounded by woodland.

"Curse ye! Ye'll pay for that!"

The sudden bellow had Beth spinning around in alarm, her heart pounding against her ribs. The clink of metal and the sound of a commotion echoed through the woods. Without thinking Beth took off towards the sound. There were people out there! They could tell her where she was and maybe give her a lift home!

As she picked her way between the thick trunks, the sounds got louder. She heard the thud of booted feet and the huff of exertion, mixed with the 'clink, clink' of metal on metal. Then she stepped into a clearing and halted in shock.

This wasn't some group of ramblers she'd stumbled on, or some tourists on a jaunt. It was a fight. In the clearing six men were engaged in a brawl. Although, brawl wasn't really the word, Beth realized. This wasn't some bar room set-to. The men were clashing with swords. Swords! Where the hell had they gotten those?

Beth gritted her teeth against the sudden panic that tried to claw up her throat. Five of the men had encircled the sixth and were attacking him mercilessly. The man spun and parried, keeping his attackers at bay with lightning reflexes, seeming to be in many places at once. The man dived under a swinging blade, went into a roll, and hammered his fist into his attacker's face as he came to his feet. The attacker staggered back, clutching at his nose, and the man laid him out with a crack to the temple that echoed like a gunshot through the wood.

The man sprang away and whirled to face the remaining four men.

"Go," he growled at them. "And I might just let ye live."

One of the attackers, a big man with arms like tree trunks, spat into the dirt. "Didnae I tell ye ye'd pay? Well, now I owe ye double. I'm gonna carve ye into chunks and leave ye for the wolves."

With a bellow the big man ran at the other, hammering him with blows so fast that Beth could hardly track them. The ring of steel on steel filled the clearing, setting Beth's teeth on edge.

The two men traded blows, moving backwards and forwards across the ground. Beth ducked behind a tree and watched in horror. The sight of such violence made her stomach churn. She abhorred violence. It was so senseless. There was *always* another way. There must be, surely? Otherwise they were no better than animals. It was one of the reasons she'd decided to become a lawyer.

The men in the clearing didn't seem to share her convictions. Even from this distance Beth could hear their grunt of effort. They weren't fooling around. As soon as one of them found a way through the other's defense, there would be serious injury—or worse.

Beth dug her cell out of her pocket again. This was definitely a matter for the police. She cursed under her breath as she saw she still had no signal. Damn it all!

In the clearing the big, roughly-dressed man was pushing back the other. Inch by slow inch, the lone man edged back towards the trees at the clearing's edge. Now that he'd come closer Beth saw he had red-blond hair that curled onto his collar and was she imagining it or was he smiling? Was this guy totally crazy?

The other attackers had been watching the fight but now they broke away, peeling off to the perimeter of the clearing. Two moved to support the big man who Beth guessed must be the leader of the gang, but the other melted into the trees, moving slowly and stealthily behind their victim.

With a growl, the blond man suddenly darted forward, allowing the big man's sword to slice through the fabric on his shoulder. The big man, surprised by this sudden change in tactics, paused and the blond man rammed his elbow into his attacker's ribs and then head-butted him hard enough to make the man's eyes roll back in his head and send him crashing to the ground.

The others closed in, stabbing viciously. Beth's hands flew to her mouth in horror but at the last moment the blond man swayed out of the way with all the reflexes of a cat, knocked the men's blades from their hands and delivered three swift uppercuts to the men's jaws that sent then cannoning into the trees before falling to the ground, unconscious.

The blond man pressed a hand to his bleeding shoulder and in that instant the remaining man—the one who'd been sneaking through the woods—struck from behind. He raised his sword high and swung it at the blond man's unprotected back.

Beth reacted instinctively. The injustice of five men attacking one made her hackles rise. The blond man might be a violent thug but that didn't mean he deserved to get skewered from behind.

"Behind you!" she bellowed.

The man's eyes flicked to Beth peering from behind the tree and widened momentarily in surprise. Then he pivoted, ducked out of the way of the sword swinging at his neck, and lunged with his own weapon, plunging it into his attacker's chest halfway to the hilt. The man's eyes widened and his sword fell from nerveless fingers. He slid off the sword that impaled him and lay lifeless in the dirt.

The blond man spun, pointing his sword in Beth's direction. "Come out."

Beth wiped a shaky hand across her brow. Oh god. He'd just killed that man! What had she walked into? She cursed her foolishness. Why had she warned him? She should have kept her mouth shut, made a run for it, and found the police. Now the blond man was staring right at her and there was nowhere to run.

She held up her hands and slowly stepped out from behind the tree. "Look, I don't want any trouble," she said, her voice a little shaky.

"Come forward."

Beth took a few steps and halted, not wanting to go any closer. His sword was smeared with blood. Beth's legs began to shake.

"Who are ye?" he demanded. "Are ye in league with these vagabonds?"

In league with them? Was he joking?

Outrage overcame her fear for a moment. "What? Are you serious? I got lost in the woods and stumbled on this...this...mess. I've never seen any of you before in my life!"

The man relaxed a little. His eyes scanned the trees. "Ye are alone?"

Beth swallowed thickly. "Yes, I'm alone." She glanced at the sword in his hand. "Please don't hurt me."

A strange look crossed the man's face. He sheathed his weapon. "Hurt ye? What do ye think I am? I dinna hurt women."

Beth pointed at the downed men. "You hurt them all right."

"They were outlaws."

"Outlaws?"

He looked her up and down. "Bad men. Men that would hurt a lass wandering the woods alone. What are ye doing here? Where are yer kin?"

"My what?"

"Yer family," he replied with a flash of annoyance. "I suggest ye get back to them. This isnae a safe place to go wandering. The laird's patrols rarely come out this far."

Beth drew in a deep breath. She struggled to follow his words. The man, she noticed, wore traditional Scottish dress: tartan plaid over a linen shirt, high boots and a sash across the chest.

He whistled and a horse came trotting out of the woods, walking up to him with a snort of greeting. The man took rope from the saddlebags and used it to bind the four unconscious men's hands then dragged them into a line in the clearing's center, along with the dead man.

"What are you doing?" Beth asked.

He glanced at her. "Would ye rather I left them free so they can attack someone else?"

"They attacked you? Why?"

"Nay, they attacked some foresters—easy pickings for men like this. I just happened to interrupt them."

"So they're criminals?"

He tested the bonds on the last man's hands and straightened. "Aye, as I've already told ye. They are outlaws. Lawless men. We are a long way from the king's protection up here."

Beth struggled to catch up. "So you're some kind of law-man? You were arresting them?"

He snorted. "Hardly. I'm a sell-sword. A mercenary. I just happen to take exception when a gang of vagabonds chooses to throw their weight around." He frowned at her. "And judging by the fact ye dinna know an outlaw when ye see one, I reckon ye are a long way from where ye are supposed to be."

You don't know the half of it, Beth thought.

She pulled in a deep breath and tried to think rationally. He'd been acting in self-defense and she knew from her train-ing that with forensic evidence and her witness testimony, the defense would probably stand up in court.

He's not a psycho, she told herself. *He's not going to kill you. He's just a man defending himself. It's okay. Breathe.*

"Do you have a cell?" she asked. "We need to call the po-lice."

He looked at her as if she'd said something ridiculous. "Cell? Police?"

"A mobile phone? I can't get a signal but if you lend me yours I'll call the police and explain what happened. I saw it all. I can tell them you were acting in self-defense. You'll be arrest-ed of course but you might get bail until your trial."

He planted his hands on his hips. "Lass, I havenae the faintest clue what ye are going on about. Have ye taken a whack on the head? I dinna ken what ye mean by 'mobile phone' or 'police.'"

Beth stared at him. Was he messing with her? Was this all some sort of sick joke? "You *are* going to report this aren't you?"

"I'll inform the Sheriff's men in Cannoch if that's what ye mean. Then these bastards will be *his* responsibility."

Beth jumped on the name. "Cannoch? Where is that?"

"Tis the nearest settlement to these parts."

Beth breathed a sigh of relief. There was a village nearby! A place where she could find a phone, call the police, and get this whole mess sorted out.

"Could you tell me how to get there?"

He wiped his sword blade on the tunic of one of the unconscious men then re-sheathed it. "I'll do better than that, lass. I'll escort ye there myself."

Beth baulked. "No, that's okay. Just give me directions and I'll find my own way." Did he really think she would go anywhere with him? After what she had just seen him do? She would not spend any more time near this man than she had to.

"Did ye not hear what I told ye?" the man said with a hint of exasperation in his voice. "Ye think these men are the only vagabonds to hide out in these woods? I canna allow ye to remain here. Ye will come with me."

Beth looked around. The wood lay still and quiet but the shadows beneath the boughs suddenly seemed menacing, as if they might be hiding enemies. Oh god. She really had no choice.

"Okay."

The man took a few steps closer and Beth resisted the urge to back away. He was tall and broad-shouldered and maybe a handful of years older than herself. A strange, swirling tattoo covered his forearm and red-gold hair framed a face of sharp cheekbones and eyes as blue as winter ice. A light dusting of stubble covered his chin. With a start she realized he was shockingly handsome.

"Where are ye from?" he asked. "Yer accent is strange."

"Seattle," she replied. "Born and bred."

"Seattle?"

"In the US?"

His eyes narrowed. "I havenae heard of such a place."

Beth breathed in deeply. Of course he'd never heard of the US. Why would she expect anything different? Just like he'd never heard of a cell phone or the police.

"Okay. Fine. Whatever. Can we get going now?" she could feel her tattered nerves beginning to fray. She needed to get back to town and some sort of sanity.

"Aye," he grunted. He turned and walked towards the horse.

"Do you have a name?" she called after him.

He turned to look over his shoulder. "Camdan MacAuley." He gathered the reins and led the horse over. "Mount up."

Beth eyed the horse. It was enormous and glared at her with undisguised malice. "You want me to ride that thing?"

"Well I dinna want ye to dance with him," Camdan snapped.

"But...but...I haven't ridden since I was six."

"Lord above, woman! It's fifteen miles to Cannoch and I'll be damned if I'm gonna walk the whole way!"

Before she could say another word he grabbed her around the waist and hoisted her into the saddle as though she was a sack of apples. Beth squawked and the horse shied at this unaccustomed weight on his back. With a gasp, she knotted her hands in the horse's mane, clinging on for dear life. Camdan reached up to steady her and then swung up behind her with practised ease.

"I'm Beth by the way," she muttered. "Thanks for asking. Bethany Carter."

He made no reply. Reaching around her to take the reins, he kicked the horse into motion. Beth squeezed her eyes shut and clung onto the saddle. Today had turned into a nightmare. Why had she ever listened to Irene damned MacAskill?

Chapter 5

C am felt ill at ease as they rode. It had turned into a very strange day. First there had been the unexpected meeting with Irene MacAskill, then the fight with the brigands, then the even more unexpected discovery of a strange lass alone in the woods—a lass who'd probably saved his life. He glanced at her perched in the saddle in front of him. There was more to her story than she was telling. She wore outlandish clothing, spoke with a strange accent and the jeweled necklace she wore suggested a noblewoman. But what would a noblewoman be doing wandering the woods alone?

It made no sense, just like most of today's events made no sense.

Firefly snorted and Cam realized he was gripping the reins tight enough to turn his knuckles white. He forced himself to relax. They'd soon reach Cannoch and then he could be rid of this unwelcome complication.

The lass sat bolt upright in the saddle, clinging to the horn in a way that suggested she was unused to riding. Her back was rigid, her shoulders tense, and she made sure to keep a gap between herself and Cam.

Despite having to circle his arms around her in order to hold the reins, Cam was careful not to touch her. She was obviously frightened of him. The look she'd given him when he insisted she rode with him had been one of pure terror. The thought sent a jolt right through his body. Who could blame her? What would she have seen when she entered that clearing? A blood-crazed mad-man?

Shame washed through him. What had happened to the man who valued his honor above all else? What had happened to the man who had stood by his brothers in countless battles and defended their clan with his life?

Gone, Cam thought. *He died on the shore that night as surely as if he took a knife through the heart.*

He'd felt nothing but exhilaration as he'd fought those brigands. The rage had demanded release, demanded violence, and Cam had given it freely. During the fight he'd been free of the ever present burning in his soul, the terrible yearning that could never be assuaged.

And when he'd killed that vagabond? When he'd driven his sword through his chest? He'd felt only triumph. What sort of man did that make him?

His father would be ashamed if he could see Camdan now. Laird David MacAuley had been a man of principle. A laird, he taught his sons, was more than just a leader. He was an example to his people, his clan. He should act with honor in all things. What honor had there been in killing that ruffian?

I didnae have a choice, he told himself. *He would have killed me.*

Such logic did nothing to assuage his guilt. Cam clenched his teeth to keep a growl from escaping. Pushing aside such thoughts, he forced himself to concentrate on their path. His eyes scanned the undergrowth and his ears strained for any sound that didn't belong. If those brigands had accomplices, they might well be tracking them by now, eager for revenge. If it came to another fight, Cam would be hard pressed to fend them off and keep the lass safe at the same time. He loosened his sword in its scabbard in readiness.

But no attack came and they soon found themselves riding out of the woodland and into the pasture land that surrounded Cannoch. Up ahead columns of chimney smoke marred the sky.

The lass sighed, almost sagging with relief.

Cam cleared his throat and spoke for the first time on the journey. "Ye have kin in Cannoch?"

She shook her head, making her long chestnut hair shimmer. When the light caught it, he could see flecks running through it like woven gold. "No. I'm staying in Banchary which I guess must be close by. In a guesthouse. I've booked a room for the weekend. My friend reckoned I needed a break." She laughed but it was a brittle sound devoid of humor. "I'm up here to relax. Funny, eh?"

"Ye live in this 'Banchary'?"

"No. I live in Edinburgh. I've been there for four years now."

Cam frowned. "But ye said ye were from...where was it? Seattle?"

"Originally. But I studied in Edinburgh. A great place to be a student. Have you been? I could recommend some places to visit if you'd like. Oh, of course you've been. You *are* Scottish after all. Sorry. I tend to prattle when I'm nervous." She clamped her mouth shut and stared straight ahead.

Cam said nothing. Her words had him more confused than ever.

They took the main trail into the settlement. To either side lay small fields carved up by withy fences. The fields held livestock: goats, chickens, pigs and the occasional plow horse. People glanced up from their work as Cam rode by, wary of strangers.

Cam guided Firefly to the small square in the village center which served as market place and meeting point. There he pulled the horse to a halt.

The lass glanced at him. "Why have we stopped?"

He gave her a puzzled frown. "We're here."

She gave him a puzzled frown of her own. "What do you mean? Where are we?"

"Where ye wanted to be. Cannoch."

Her eyes widened. "Cannoch? You seriously think I'm that stupid? Okay, joke over. Where are we really? This looks like some historical re-enactment type place."

He swung his leg over the saddle and jumped to the ground. "Why would ye think this a joke? Ye asked to go to Cannoch and that's where I've brought ye. The inn is over there."

He nodded to the far side of the square then held up his hand to help her down. She eyed him warily for a moment then gingerly reached out and took his hand. Her skin felt warm and soft and her hand seemed impossibly small in his. He glanced up and found her looking down at him. Her eyes were as deep a brown as freshly tilled earth.

Feeling suddenly uncomfortable, Cam cleared his throat. "Swing yer leg over the horse's back and jump down. I willnae let ye fall."

She followed his instructions but was so ungainly that Cam was glad she wore trews like a man, otherwise the whole street would have gained a view of her backside. She slid to the ground and Cam caught her, his hands going reflexively round her waist. She stumbled and caught herself, her fingers gripping his forearms.

"Easy, lass. We dinna want ye falling face-first in the dirt."

"Now wouldn't that just round off a damn-fine day?" she muttered. She steadied herself and then looked up at him. "Thanks."

Her eyes met his. She had a slight dusting of freckles across her nose and a dimple in her chin. His breath quickened. Lord above, she was beautiful.

He stepped back quickly. "This way."

He grabbed Firefly's reins and marched across the square, not bothering to see if the lass followed. After a moment, she caught up with him.

Her head swiveled from side to side as they walked, her eyes wide. From the look on her face, anyone would think she'd never seen a village before. Probably used to fancy manor houses or castles.

They reached the village's only inn. It was a ramshackle place built on the crossroads that brought Cannoch its trade. Its lower floor was constructed of stone, the upper, timber, with a roof of worn-out thatch over the top.

The door hung open and from inside came the sound of someone playing a fiddle. He tied Firefly to the post outside then led the way inside. Pipe smoke filled the air and from out the back came the smell of roasting meat. Camdan's growling stomach reminded him that he hadn't eaten since this morning but he didn't have time for a meal now. If he wanted to reach the northern road by sundown, he needed to be on his way.

Beside him, the lass stared wide-eyed around, her face pale.

"Dinna worry," he said. "Ye'll be safe now—as long as ye keep out of the woods."

She gulped and looked up at him. "What the hell is this place?"

"I've already told ye," he replied, stifling a stab of impatience. Was she deliberately trying to annoy him? "Ye said ye wanted to go to the nearest settlement. This is it."

BETH STARED AT HIM. He was kidding, right? Whatever the hell this place was, it most definitely was *not* a tourist village, and this was most definitely not a hotel. The room had plain wooden floorboards strewn with rushes, unlit candles sitting on the rickety tables, and thick beams holding up the roof. It looked like something out of a history book.

She looked around slowly. All the patrons were wearing the same traditional dress as Camdan although the tartan of their plaids were different colors. Except for a young woman weaving between the tables carrying pewter tankards on a tray, all the customers appeared to be men.

A terrifying suspicion began to form in her mind. Everyone wore plaid and carried weapons. Cannoch was little more than a rustic village. Camdan looked at her as if she was crazy every time she asked him to use his cell phone. The pieces suddenly clicked into place and the implications made her stagger with sudden dizziness. She placed a hand on the wall to steady herself.

"What's wrong?" Camdan asked, coming immediately to her side. "Lass?"

She breathed deeply, trying to calm her suddenly hammering pulse. No. No, no, no. It couldn't be. It was impossible. *Impossible!*

Looking up at Camdan she forced words through a constriction in her throat. "What...what year is this?"

He stared at her as if she'd gone daft. "Have ye lost yer wits, woman? What kind of question is that?"

"Answer me!" she snapped.

Camdan scowled at her sharp tone. "King James has sat the throne for twenty eight years. It's 1542, of course."

1542.

Oh god. Oh holy god. That's why everything was so strange. She wasn't in the wrong place at all.

She was in the wrong time.

The edges of her vision went fuzzy and for a moment she feared she might pass out. Gritting her teeth, she dragged a ragged breath into her lungs, closed her eyes for a moment and forced aside the dizziness. No. She would *not* faint. She would figure this the hell out.

Camdan stepped close. "Lass? Are ye well?"

Glancing at him, she felt a hysterical laugh bubbling in her chest. *Well? Of course! I'm just dandy! I've only been whipped back in time by several centuries. No skin off my nose.*

Oh hell. Oh bloody hell fire.

The room suddenly felt claustrophobic. She had to get away. Away from Camdan, away from the inn, away from all of it. She spun on her heel and marched out into the street. The late afternoon sun cast ribbons of light through the clouds that were gathering to the west and the breeze had picked up, sending her hair streaming out behind her.

Beth pressed a shaky hand to her forehead and forced her addled brain to think.

I'm hallucinating, she told herself. *That's the only explanation. Or I've hit my head and I'm dreaming. This is not real. It can't be. This is not real!*

She would find the road or a cell signal or a phone box and call the police. Then she would return to the guesthouse in Banchary and forget any of this had happened. Of course she would.

Digging her nails into her palms to steady herself, Beth lifted her chin, pulled in a breath, and marched off down the road.

CAMDAN STOOD IN THE street and watched the lass go. She walked with purpose, as if she knew her destination but her behaviour at the inn suggested otherwise. For a moment in there he'd been sure she was going to swoon.

He shook his head. The woman was obviously unhinged. She talked about things he'd never heard of and acted strangely. He knew of no other woman who would have risked herself to warn him of that brigand. She was brave to the point of recklessness and yet seemed uneasy at the mere sight of his sword or the blood on the dead man's chest.

Squinting against the glare of the lowering sun, he watched her until she disappeared into the distance. Good. He was well rid of her. She was a complication he didn't need. Pausing only long enough to send word to the sheriff about the brigands he'd left in the woods, he untied Firefly and climbed into the saddle.

The stallion snorted and stamped, as eager as his master to be on his way. Yet Cam hesitated. He ought to pull Firefly around and trot out of the village the other way, heading north where he might be able to pick up work in some lord's garrison. With winter coming on, hired guards were always in demand against the rise in banditry the harsh season inevitably caused. Aye, he should ride away and forget the lass. He owed her nothing. Hadn't he brought her safely to Cannoch as he'd promised? Any debt between them was settled.

But he didn't move. His father's training took hold. The lass was disorientated and alone. Any man with a shred of honor wouldn't leave her to her fate on the road.

But I'm not a man of honor, he told himself. *Not anymore. I'm a hired sword, killing for the highest bidder. What use are a laird's notions of honor to me?*

Firefly whinnied and shook out his mane, snorting at the delay. The sun was sinking towards the horizon and it would soon be sunset.

"Ah! Damnation!" he growled.

Cursing his own stupidity, he nudged Firefly into a trot after the lass.

Chapter 6

Beth tramped along the road, keeping her eyes peeled for anything that looked familiar. A road-sign, an isolated cottage, hell, even the streak of a plane through the sky would have reassured her that she wasn't going totally crazy. Banchary wasn't that far from Edinburgh. With night coming on, the lights of the great city should have lit the sky for miles around. But there was nothing. Just the undulating landscape and the muddy track she followed.

It would be dark soon and then what would she do? Walking out of Cannoch suddenly seemed like a stupid idea. Maybe she ought to return and see if Camdan was still there. He was the only familiar thing in a suddenly shaky world.

But the stubborn part of her refused to entertain the idea. If she returned there, it was like she was admitting she'd traveled through time. Her brain just wouldn't accept that, not until she'd exhausted all other possibilities. And besides, Camdan scared her. He was exactly the kind of mindless thug she'd vowed to help put away. Why would she want to spend any more time near that man?

She broke into a jog, determined that over the next rise she'd see the lights of cars snaking through the valley below or spot the glow of Edinburgh in the distance. She found neither.

When she reached the top of the hill all that met her eyes was a sea of trees clinging to the lower slopes of heather-clad hills.

Panic tinged her thoughts now and she found herself picking up the pace until she was pelting along the muddy track, her boots splashing through puddles and throwing up clods of earth. Soon her lungs were burning and she slowed to a stop, leaning over and catching her breath. All around were the darkening woods. The squawking cry of a pheasant cut through the air but other than that, all was still.

Beth straightened and rifled through her pockets. She came up with a stick of chewing gum, her cell phone, a pack of tissues and Irene's flyer about the Castle View Guesthouse. With a growl, she crunched it into a ball and threw it away with all her might.

Damn Irene MacAskill! And damn herself for listening to her!

She needed shelter. The temperature would drop considerably once it got dark and there was the smell of rain in the air. She left the trail and forged into the woods, looking for somewhere she could hunker down for the night: a cottage would be best but even a cave would do! But as she walked, eyes scanning the landscape, the ground suddenly gave way beneath her feet. With a scream, Beth plunged downwards only to hit solid stone and be thrown to her knees a second later.

She scrabbled up. Natural stone walls rose on either side of her, slimy with rotted leaf litter. She seemed to have fallen down some sort of ravine, a narrow cut through the forest floor that had been hidden by dead wood and leaves. The ravine was not deep, maybe ten feet, but the walls were too high for her to jump and grab the edge.

Grabbing hold of two protruding rocks, Beth tried to climb out, but the rocks were so slippery she couldn't keep a grip and she slithered back down to the bottom. Tears of frustration welled in her eyes. She pounded her fists against the rock.

"This is not fair!" she screamed at the top of her voice. "Irene, I'm going to kill you!"

The sound echoed off the walls and shattered the silence of the night. Only when it died away did she realize it was probably not a good idea to shout like that. Camdan had warned her there might be more outlaws around and she was very, very sure she didn't want any of them stumbling upon her in the night.

She bit her lip to keep in her emotions and pulled her coat tighter around her neck. The autumn night carried a chill that spoke of the winter to come and Beth's teeth began to chatter. With a sigh she slid down the wall and sat with her knees against her chest. Her head drooped, her forehead coming to rest against her knees.

She was starting to drowse when a sudden noise startled her from her doze. She sat bolt upright and went very still, her heart thundering. It came again: the soft rustle of footsteps in the leaf litter.

A jolt of pure terror went through her. She looked around desperately, searching for some place to run but there was nowhere to go. She was caught like a rat in a trap. She grabbed a fallen branch and held it out with both hands like a club. Let them come! She'd be damned if she'd go down without a fight!

Light flared above her as someone leaned over with a flaming brand. Beth squinted, throwing up her arm against the sudden light. She blinked in surprise. The figure that peered down at her wasn't the rough outlaw she'd expected. It was Camdan MacAuley.

"Lass?" he called. "Is that ye down there?"

Beth almost wept with relief. Her legs turned shaky and she leaned against the wall for support. "Yes! Be careful, the leaf litter on the edge is slippery."

He crouched. "Ye seem to have a knack for getting yerself into trouble, lass."

She laughed shakily. "Trouble? Me? Nah. I was just taking in the view down here."

A faint smile passed over his face. He held the flaming brand high, inspecting the walls of the cut.

"Wait there," he instructed.

He disappeared then returned a moment later holding a coil of rope.

"Wrap this around yer waist and tie the end. I'll pull ye up."

Beth caught the end of the rope as it came snaking down then followed his instructions, knotting it round her waist. Camdan took up the slack.

"Try to brace yer hands and feet against the wall as I hoist ye up and look for hand and footholds to help ye. Are ye ready?"

Beth placed her hands on the ravine wall and nodded. "Ready."

Camdan braced the rope around his hips and began to pull. Inch by slow inch, Beth was hauled up. The rope bit painfully into her middle and she had to grit her teeth against the discomfort, but she did her best to climb, finding hand and footholds where she could, taking the weight from the creaking rope where possible. Camdan gritted his teeth and the muscles in his arms bulged as he strained, passing the rope through his hands bit by bit.

The climb seemed to take forever but at last Beth reached the top. Camdan grabbed her arm and pulled her over. She collapsed against him and suddenly tears came flooding out. Tears of relief and frustration and fear. She buried her face in his shoulder, suddenly unable to hold back the flood of emotions that she'd kept in check all day. Her body shook with sobs.

Camdan's arms went around her, holding her tight, and they felt strong and reassuring.

"Easy, lass. It's all right. I've got ye."

She sucked in a heaving breath and stepped back, suddenly embarrassed. She wiped at her eyes and then untied the rope from around her waist.

"Thanks," she muttered in a hoarse voice. "I guess I owe you one."

"Nay, lass," he replied. "Now we are even. I reckon that brigand might have skewered me if ye hadnae warned me he was there."

"I couldn't let him sneak up on you like that. It was hardly fair." She looked up at him. "What are you doing here? I thought you had somewhere to be."

He shrugged. "Nowhere that canna wait. Mayhap I have a nose for trouble too. What were ye thinking of, lass, storming off like that? It isnae safe to wander alone at night."

"I wasn't thinking at all," she replied. "I just needed..." She threw up her hands. "Oh, I don't know what I needed. I'm just glad you came along."

"Aye, well its too dark to travel back to Cannoch now. We'll have to camp here."

Beth followed him through the woods to a small clearing sheltered on one side by a shelf of rock tangled with holly bushes. In this clearing Camdan's horse had been tethered. The beast stood with his head hanging, drowsing, but came alert as his master entered the clearing, snorting in greeting and pricking his ears forward.

Camdan gave the stallion a pat on the nose and then crossed to where he'd piled the saddlebags, replacing the coiled rope inside.

Now that she noticed, she saw that Camdan carried a lot of gear. The saddlebags bulged and were hung with all sorts of things that indicated a life spent outdoors. He crouched and pulled out a blanket which he tossed to Beth then bade her sit down on a log in the clearing's center. Too exhausted to object, Beth did as she was told.

Cam walked around the clearing collecting branches and twigs and then, with the calm efficiency of someone who'd done this countless times before, started a fire. Beth was grateful for the warmth and reached her hands out to the merrily crackling blaze.

"Are ye hungry?" Cam asked.

"Starving," Beth replied. "I think I could eat a horse."

"I willnae tell Firefly ye said that," Cam replied with the ghost of a smile. "He's a most sensitive beast."

Firelight danced in his eyes and his smile was warm. He seemed a different man to the cold, ruthless killer she'd met this afternoon. She'd thought him a callous brute but would such a man have come after her like this? Saved her from the ravine? Her eyes settled on the tattoo that covered his forearm. The design of interlocking coils was similar to the markings she'd seen on the walls of the ruins where she'd entered this time. Coincidence?

He noticed her looking and a strange look crossed his face. "I'll find us something to eat," he said abruptly before stalking over to the saddlebags and returning with two large, dry biscuits.

"I only have hardtack."

"Hardtack?" she said, taking the offered biscuit with a smile. "My favorite. Thanks."

She began eating. It was rock-hard and as dry as sandpaper but to Beth it tasted like heaven. Camdan settled on a log on the other side of the fire. He took a swig from a flask and then tossed it to Beth. She set the flask to her lips, took a long pull, then broke into a fit of coughing. She'd expected water but the liquid in the flask burned her mouth like acid.

"Easy, lass," Camdan said. "Ye are supposed to sip whisky, not gulp it like a dying woman."

"Whisky?" Beth blurted. "Bloody hell! You could have warned me! It tastes like battery acid!"

He nodded. "Aye. Maybe not the best vintage but Cannoch isnae known for its distillery. Still, it keeps out the cold."

"Yeah, it certainly does that," Beth replied, pressing a hand to her stomach.

Silence fell, interrupted only by the crackling of the fire. Beth felt weary to her bones. Sleep tugged at her but she fought to stay awake. There was so much she needed to know if she was ever going to figure out what had happened to her and how to fix it. Starting with her rescuer.

"You seem to know the land around here pretty well," she said. "You're local?"

He shook his head, his red-gold hair glinting in the fire-light. "Nay. My family's lands lie to the south west, many miles distant. I havenae been there in a long time."

His voice trailed off and he stared into the fire. Beth suspected there was more to that story but she didn't push it.

"What about ye, lass?" he asked. "How did ye end up in the woods alone? Having a noble lady come to my aid against a group of armed brigands was a mighty shock, I can tell ye."

"I'm not a noble lady," she replied. "I'm just a barista."

He gave her a puzzled look and she bit back a curse. She had to be careful what she said. The last thing she wanted was to let him know the truth about where she'd come from. He might have rescued her but that didn't mean she would trust him with something like that. Who knew how he would react to such a claim?

"I...um...that is..." she thought furiously, trying to come up with a credible explanation. "I've just finished studying to become a lawyer."

"A lawyer?" he said. "But ye are a woman. Tis only men that study such things."

"Yeah?" Beth replied, raising an eyebrow. "Well, things are a little different where I come from."

"Aye," he said, eyeing her jeans, boots and coat. "I can see that. But that still doesnae explain what ye were doing in the woods alone." The look he fixed her with was piercing. He wouldn't be put off by any of her vague explanations. "Where are yer kin, lass?"

Beth sucked in a breath. She really didn't want to talk about this. Why was he asking her so many questions? "What have my family got to do with anything?"

His expression hardened. "Because it is mighty strange for a woman to be traveling alone, that's what. Dinna ye have men folk to protect ye? A husband? Brothers? Father?"

No! she wanted to shout. *I don't have any of that!* Instead, she groped for an explanation that would satisfy him.

"I went to Banchary because I was invited by a woman I met in Edinburgh. Once I was there I met her by some ruins. Then I stepped through an arch and I think I might have passed out for a while. When I came around she was gone."

Cam raised an eyebrow. "And did this woman have a name?"

"She was called Irene. Irene MacAskill."

Cam froze, his hand raised half-way to his mouth. "Did ye say Irene MacAskill?"

Beth sat up straighter. "Yes! Do you know her?"

"Nay, I dinna *know* her," he replied. "But I met a woman by that name today, only a few hours before I encountered ye."

"Then she might still be around here!" Beth said, suddenly excited. "Maybe we could find her!" It was the first piece of good news she'd had all day. If Irene had brought her to this time it stood to reason that the old woman would be able to send her back as well.

"Aye. Maybe," Cam replied doubtfully. He finished his biscuit and then stood, brushing crumbs off his plaid. He crossed to the saddlebags and pulled out a bedroll which he laid by Beth's feet. "Get some sleep. We will talk more in the morning."

Beth glanced at the bedroll and then at the saddlebags. "Where's your bedroll?"

He shrugged. "I only have the one. Dinna worry about me. I have my cloak."

Beth opened her mouth to protest but a huge yawn took her.

"Sleep, Beth," Cam said. "That's an order."

She looked up sharply. That was the first time he'd used her name. The sound of him speaking it sent a quiver right through her. He looked down at her for a moment, firelight dancing in his eyes, before stepping back and retreating to his spot across the fire.

With a sigh Beth laid herself down on the leather mat and pulled the blanket tight around her. She watched the dancing flames for a moment but the weariness soon rose up and pulled her into dreamless slumber.

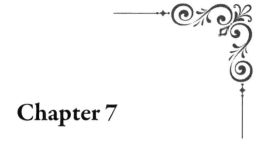

Chapter 7

Cam settled on the log, took out his whetstone, and began sharpening one of the many daggers he kept around his person. The familiar metallic rasp and the rhythmic, mindless task usually helped to calm his turbulent thoughts. But not tonight.

Beth had met Irene MacAskill, the same woman who'd appeared to him and told him there was a way to change his destiny. Could it be coincidence? Hardly. The old woman wasn't an old woman at all, he was sure of it. Why were the Fae still plaguing him? Hadn't he given them enough? Hadn't trading his life satisfied them? It seemed not.

He tested the edge of the dagger against his thumb. It was sharp enough to draw blood. He sheathed it and took out the next, setting the edge of the whetstone against the blade and running it along the metal in smooth strokes.

He glanced down at the tattoo that marked his forearm. The swirling black coils caught the firelight in a way that made them almost look alive. They were a constant reminder of what he'd become.

Of what he'd lost.

He closed his eyes for a moment and remembered another night like this one, a lifetime ago now, when he and his brothers had entered into the bargain that doomed them all. Why had they trusted the Fae? Why had they thought they could strike a deal with such creatures?

We didnae have a choice, he reminded himself.

A branch popped in the fire and Cam looked up, startled from his thoughts. Beth was asleep, curled up on the bed roll, sleeping the deep slumber of the exhausted. Who was she? She avoided his questions deftly, revealing nothing about her background.

Right now, she looked peaceful. A stray strand of dark hair had fallen across her face and Cam resisted the urge to brush it away. She was still wary of him and the last thing he wanted to do was give her a reason to be.

When had he started to care what she thought? She was nothing more than a complication he didn't need. He was better rid of her. Wasn't he?

Then why did ye come after her? he asked himself. *Why not ride away and leave her to her fate?*

Cam sighed. It had been a long day and his body ached for sleep. He placed his sword on the ground next to him in case he should need it quickly, then lay down on the cold ground, as close to the fire as he could safely get, and rolled himself into his cloak. He fell quickly into slumber, his dreams plagued by images of two women: one old with iron-gray hair, the other young with large eyes and a laughing smile.

BETH WOKE WITH A START. She bolted upright, foggy confusion filling her brain as she found herself surrounded by trees rather than the familiar comfort of her bedroom. Then, as her thoughts cleared, yesterday's events came crashing in with enough force to make her stomach turn over.

Of course. She wasn't in her apartment. She wasn't in Edinburgh. Hell, she wasn't even in her *time*!

She clenched her teeth, determined not to let the panic of yesterday rule her thoughts. Today was a day for action. For figuring out exactly what she must do to get home.

"Good morning, lass," said a voice.

She spun around to find Camdan MacAuley sitting on his log across the embers of last night's fire. A pan of water sat in those embers, just starting to come to the boil. Cam's ice-blue eyes looked her over.

"Good morning," she mumbled.

She scrambled out of the blanket and climbed to her feet, stretching her arms over her head to work out the kinks and aches that sleeping on the hard ground had left.

It would soon be dawn and although it would be a little while yet before the sun rose high enough to crest the tops of the trees, light filtered through the trunks, making the dew on the leaves sparkle like tiny diamonds. A little way off Firefly was busy munching on the bushes that clustered close to the base of the rock face and a blackbird nosed around in the leaf litter. The air smelled clean and fresh.

Cam used a forked stick to lift the pan from the fire and then poured the water into two small pottery beakers. He tossed in something taken from a pouch then held one of the beakers up to Beth.

"I promise it isnae whisky this time."

"Shame," Beth said with a smile. "I was just getting used to it."

She took the beaker and lifted it to her lips, taking a sip. To her surprise and delight she found that it was camomile tea.

"Ah, that's good," she said, sitting down on the other log and holding the warm mug between her hands. "Although I'd prefer an espresso." When Cam looked at her quizzically she quickly added, "Never mind. Just something we drink in my homeland."

Cam rummaged in the saddlebags and produced another biscuit of hardtack which he tossed over to her. She took it with a nod of thanks and began eating. Cam stared into the flames, seemingly lost in thought.

Beth finished her tea and biscuit and stood up. She crossed over to Camdan and stuck out her hand.

"Thank you for all your help. I won't forget it."

He stood, took her hand with a slightly bemused expression on his face, and shook it. Beth couldn't help but notice how big and warm his hands were, his skin hard and calloused from holding a sword.

"Ye are welcome, lass," he rumbled. "What will ye do now?"

Ah, that was the question, wasn't it? She could think of only one course of action.

"I'm going back to Banchary. From there I hope to find a way home."

She'd thought about this. She reasoned that if she could walk back through the original arch, the one in Banchary, it would take her home. The archway must be some sort of portal and all she had to do was return to her portal of origin. Or, so she hoped.

Cam frowned. "Banchary? I havenae heard of it."

Beth waved a hand. "It's a little village. About five miles outside Edinburgh?"

His frowned deepened. "Edinburgh is a long way off, lass."

"What do you mean? No it isn't. It's just a few miles to the west. I can probably walk there in a couple of hours if you point me in the right direction.

Cam stared at her as if she'd sprouted two heads. "Lass," he said slowly. "Do ye know where ye are? Ye are in the Highlands. Edinburgh is over a hundred miles to the south."

It was Beth's turn to stare. Her stomach clenched. A hundred miles? She felt the blood drain from her face. Oh god. Not only had Irene's arch brought her through time, it had transported her across the country!

Cam watched her in silence for a moment, his blue eyes thoughtful. Then he drew in a breath. "I will escort ye there."

Beth blinked. "What? Why would you do that? You don't owe me anything."

"Must it be a debt?" he said, a little sharply. "I'm a MacAuley and on my honor, I couldnae allow ye to wander off alone."

"But...but...I thought you were looking for work as a mercenary?" she protested.

He shrugged. "There will be plenty of work in Edinburgh. Mayhap I should try my luck in the city."

He gazed down at her and Beth found herself unable to look away. His eyes were the lightest, clearest blue she'd ever seen, like frost covering a winter pond.

"I will keep ye safe, Bethany Carter," he said in a rough voice. "I swear on my clan's name."

She opened her mouth to speak, but no words came out. Who was this man? And why did his nearness make the skin on the back of her neck tingle?

She cleared her throat. "I...um...thanks."

He nodded then began repacking the saddlebags.

Beth took a deep breath. Okay. She had a plan. From Edinburgh she would be able to find Banchary and the archway. All would be well.

She rolled up the sleeping mat then rinsed out the cups. In silence she and Cam worked together to break camp and it seemed no time at all before she was mounted in front of him and they were riding out of the clearing and down onto the road.

"We'll need supplies," Cam said behind her. "It's a long road and we'll have to cross the mountains. We'll visit Netherlay—we should be able to get everything we need there."

Cam nudged Firefly into a walk and they began their journey.

BETH LOOKED AROUND as they traveled, trying to take in all the details and filing them away in her memory. You never knew when something might come in useful.

The landscape was beautiful. The road snaked its way through a series of undulating valleys. More often than not a stream wound its way along the valley's base and the road followed its course, the bubbling water adding its music to the sounds of the day. They seemed to be climbing higher as they traveled. Whenever they crested a rise she could see the snow capped flanks of mountains in the distance and they seemed to be getting steadily closer.

The weather held fair, for which Beth was profoundly grateful, and she found herself beginning to relax. Cam was mostly silent but he occasionally spoke to point out a landmark or some of the local wildlife. Whenever she glanced back at him she found his eyes continually scanning the terrain, as though on the lookout for danger. Beth shivered, remembering Cam running his sword through the outlaw's chest.

Towards mid-morning the trees peeled back and they found themselves traveling through the tilled fields that surrounded a settlement. It was bigger than Cannoch and the inn at the center was in better repair, its thatched roof freshly replaced and a brightly painted sign outside.

Cam pulled Firefly to a halt outside and dismounted. He held up a hand to help Beth dismount and then tossed the reins to a stable boy who came running from around the back.

"This way," he said to Beth.

Without waiting for an answer, he went inside. The inn's common room was large and well kept. The floorboards had been polished to a shine and large bunches of dried flowers hung from the beams, giving it a pleasant smell. A few of the tables were occupied—merchants by the look of the well-dressed men—and they turned to look up as Cam and Beth entered but quickly looked away when faced with Cam's belligerent glare.

A middle-aged woman with long red hair coiled in a plait came hurrying over.

"Good day," she said cheerfully. "What can I do for ye? Food? Drink? A room for the night?"

"Aye," Cam replied. "To all three although a room where the lady may bathe and change is the most pressing. Ale and food later after I have completed some errands."

"Of course," the woman smiled. "If ye will follow me, my lady." She walked over to the stairs and waited expectantly for Beth to follow.

"What about you?" Beth said to Cam. "Where are you going?"

"To buy supplies," he replied curtly, his eyes scanning the patrons of the inn. He seemed surly, on edge. "I willnae be long."

Beth caught his arm. "Wait."

She pulled the sapphire necklace from around her neck. It had been a present for her eighteenth birthday and she hardly ever took it off. It was one of the few reminders she kept of her parents. She sucked in a breath then held it out to Cam.

He frowned. "What's that for?"

"Payment. Use it to buy supplies."

The frown became a scowl and he looked suddenly offended. "Did I ask for payment, lass?" he snapped. "Do ye think I offered ye aid for money?"

"No," she snapped back, annoyed in turn. "But I'll be damned if I don't pay my way!" He opened his mouth as if to speak but she continued before he could. "And don't say a word about your god-damned honor! Take the necklace!"

He stared at her for a moment and she stared right back, the necklace dangling from her fist between them. His jaw tightened and for a second she thought he was going to argue, but then he snatched the necklace, whirled, and stormed out of the inn.

Beth sighed. Behind her the innkeeper cleared her throat. "If ye are ready, my lady, I'll show ye to a room."

If she'd heard the altercation between her and Cam, the woman said nothing of it but she did eye Beth's clothes and she was reminded again of how alien this place was. In her twenty-first century jeans and shirt she must stick out like a sore thumb.

She followed the innkeeper up two flights of stairs to a room at the back. It was built into the eaves and large beams crossed the ceiling. White plaster covered the walls and a thick rug hid most of the floor, woven in a pattern similar to the tartan the woman wore. An inglenook fireplace, big enough for Beth to stand in filled one wall and a large bed took up the center of the room. To Beth's delight, a large metal bathtub stood in front of the fire.

Seeing her eyeing it, the innkeeper smiled. "Would ye like me to get the girls to heat water for ye?"

"Would you? That would be amazing. Thanks!"

The woman nodded. "Well, I'll leave ye to it. I'll send the girls up as soon as the water's boiled but be sure to give me a shout if ye need anything."

"I will."

After the woman had left Beth kicked off her coat and boots and threw herself onto the bed. Staring up at the ceiling, she blew out a long breath. It felt good to lie down. From downstairs came the sound of mumbled conversation and the clink of crockery. Normal sounds. Every day sounds.

She closed her eyes, meaning to rest for only a moment, but she soon found herself drifting into a doze. She was awoken a little while later by a knock on the door. She sprang off the bed and answered the door to find two young women holding buckets waiting outside.

One of them gave a curtsey. "Thelma sent us to fill yer bath, my lady."

"Of course," Beth said, pulling the door wide. "Please come in."

The girls quickly filled the bathtub. They worked in silence but Beth caught the glances they flicked in her direction. She got the uneasy feeling that gossip about a strange outland woman who dressed like a man was already starting to filter through the village. Shit. She really needed to fit in a little better than this.

When they'd finished filling the tub one of the girls said, "Would ye like us to help ye bathe, my lady?"

Beth blinked at them. Help her bathe? "Um, no. Thanks. I'll be fine."

The girls shared a glance. Then they gave another curtsey and left the room.

Beth stripped off her clothing, wincing a little as the cool air played across her skin, and made her way over to the tub. The water temperature was just right and she found a bar of lavender scented soap and some large cloths to use as towels. She stepped in and allowed herself to sink down until the water covered her from chin to toes, reveling in the luxurious feel of the hot water against her skin.

She closed her eyes, allowing the heat to work the tension out of her muscles. Then, when she'd soaked long enough to begin to feel relaxed, she took the lavender soap and cleaned herself thoroughly. As she washed away the grime from spending a night in the woods, she felt some of her anxiety wash away as well. She might be five hundred years in the past but some things still felt like home. It was amazing how a good soak could do wonders.

She only climbed out of the bath when the water began to grow tepid. She wound one of the large cloths around herself and tied up her hair with the other then eyed her clothes gingerly. She didn't relish the thought of putting the dirty garments back on.

She was startled from her thoughts by a knock on the door. "Who is it?" she called.

"Mrs MacAndrew, my dear. May I come in?"

"Sure, the door's open."

The innkeeper entered and smiled at Beth. "I hope that's made ye feel better, my dear. I always feel refreshed after a long hot bath."

"You can say that again. I feel almost human."

The woman smiled. "Yer husband has just returned. He's waiting in the common room but asked me to bring ye this."

Husband? With a start Beth realized she must mean Camdan. She felt a blush suffuse her cheeks. Shit, she had to remember that attitudes in this time were very different to the twenty-first century. Seeing as they were staying at an inn together, the innkeeper would naturally assume she and Cam were married. It was probably best not to disabuse her of that notion.

"Did he?" she asked. "What is it?"

The woman held out her arm and Beth saw that she had a dress draped over it. It looked like something straight out of a medieval saga. Long, flowing, with tight sleeves and a bodice decorated with tiny embroidered flowers, Beth had to admit that it was beautiful. Her blush deepened. Cam had bought that for her?

"Oh," she stammered, taking the dress. "Thanks for bringing it up. I'll change and be down in a moment."

The woman hovered as though she wanted to ask questions but when Beth wasn't forthcoming, she smiled and left. Beth held the dress up. It looked about the right size and had hooks up the back to fasten it. She stepped into it then instantly regretted letting the innkeeper leave. The hooks were a nightmare and Beth struggled to reach behind herself and do them all up.

But finally she had the dress on and she brushed it down, looking herself over. It fitted perfectly and made a swishing noise when she moved. There were no shoes so she donned her boots but luckily the dress was long enough to cover them. She tied her old clothes into a bundle then used the wooden comb laid out by the bathtub to brush her hair. It lay in messy tangles on her shoulders and she wished fervently for a hairdryer. There was no mirror in the room but Beth guessed she looked ridiculous. Dresses had never suited her. Still, if she was going to fit in here, she couldn't worry about the vagaries of sixteenth-century fashions.

Finally ready, Beth crossed to the door, drew in a deep breath, then strode down the stairs to the common room. It had filled up during the afternoon and now most of the tables were occupied. She noticed there was an empty space surrounding the table where Camdan sat. A mug sat on the table in front of him and he'd drawn his dagger and was slowly running a whetstone up and down its surface, the grate of it cutting through the hubbub in the room like nails on slate.

His shoulders were hunched and he had a scowl on his face that could curdle milk. He radiated tension, a fact obviously not lost on the patrons, who were all giving him a wide berth. The bottom step creaked as Beth stepped into the room and Cam looked up. His eyes widened as they alighted on her and she felt heat creep into her cheeks.

He looked away and returned to sharpening his dagger. She crossed the common room and sat down opposite him. He glanced at her and away again, offering no word of greeting.

"Thanks," she said. "For the dress."

"Yer clothing marked ye as an outlander," he replied. "Trews and boots may be fit for a lass where yer from but here all they will do is draw attention."

The innkeeper approached laden with a tray of steaming food. She placed two plates on the table along with a pewter tankard of ale. A basket of bannocks followed. Beth smiled and thanked her but Cam didn't look up from sharpening his dagger. With a shrug, Beth began tucking into the food.

After a moment, Cam put his dagger away and began picking at his plate. His gaze, Beth noticed, wandered constantly over the common room. What was wrong with him? He'd been as edgy as a spooked cat ever since they'd ridden into town. What was it about this place that had him so freaked?

She was about to ask him when he suddenly spoke. "I've purchased supplies. We'll stay here for tonight and leave at first light. Ye will take the room, I'll sleep in the stable. Get a good night's sleep—it will be the last bed ye'll sleep in for a while."

Beth nodded. As they ate she did her best to make conversation but Cam's surly demeanour was like a wall she couldn't breach. When she asked questions she received one-word answers and when she tried to engage him in banter she received only a grunt. After a while she gave up and concentrated on the meal.

The door suddenly opened and three men walked into the common room. They paused by the door, looking around. Their eyes settled on Cam and they sauntered over to their table.

"Here he is!" one of them said. "So it's true! Ye *are* back in town, ye wily old bastard!"

The room, Beth noticed, had suddenly gone deathly quiet. A prickle of unease walked down her spine. These men were richly dressed yet something about the feral looks in their eyes reminded Beth of the outlaws they'd encountered in the woods.

Cam pushed his plate away and looked up. "Aye. Here I am." His voice was quiet but even so it seemed to carry through the room like a cold breeze. "What do ye want, Marley?"

Marley grinned, showing a gap where his front teeth ought to be. "Aye, that's the warm greeting we've come to expect from the mighty Camdan MacAuley. What are ye doing in these parts? I'd heard ye'd gone north. Didnae think ye'd be fool enough to come this way again."

"That's my business," Cam grated.

Marley grinned then turned to his two fellows. "I was just telling Bain and Kye here of yer exploits. They didnae believe half of them, of course. Care to prove them wrong? MacGregor is looking for men. He's been like a bear with a sore tooth since ye left. Never got over losing his best fighter. I'm sure he'd be pleased to have ye back."

"I dinna give two shits what MacGregor does or doesnae think," Cam replied. "I'm done with that."

"Done with it?" Marley said. The friendly tone was gone and now his voice growled with menace. "Ye'll never be done with it. It's what ye are, Demon Blade." His eyes flicked to Beth and his look turned calculating. "Found yerself a doxy, have ye? Mayhap that's why ye are too afraid to fight."

Cam surged to his feet, sending his chair toppling over backwards. In a flash, so fast that Beth barely registered the movement, he grabbed Marley by his shirt and pressed the tip of his dagger against the man's throat.

"Ye will learn some manners," Cam said, his voice the more chilling for its calmness. "Even if I have to carve it into ye. And ye should know by now that I'm never afraid to fight."

The room had gone quiet as a grave. Beth watched in wide-eyed horror, hardly daring to breathe. Marley's companions burst into action, breaking the tableau. One of them swung a fist at the back of Cam's head. He ducked and the blow went over his head and smashed into Marley's nose instead. Marley grunted and staggered back into the table, sending the dinner plates flying.

With a yelp Beth sprang out of the way as Marley crashed to the floor. Cam spun to face his attacker, landing a punch into his ribs and then, as he doubled-over, hitting him square on the chin. The man staggered back, eyes rolling in his head, and slowly slithered down the wall to the floor.

That left the third man. The commotion had given him time to draw his sword and now he came at Camdan with a savage thrust. Cam swayed out of the way just in time and the blade pierced the place where he'd been standing. The man recovered quickly, following Cam with a riposte. Cam met his swing with his dagger, catching the larger blade on the smaller. For a moment they were locked, Cam's teeth bared and his arms straining as he fought to hold the sword away from his face. Then Cam lashed out with his foot, kicking the man hard in the knee. The man crashed to the ground with a cry of pain, his sword clattering to the floorboards.

Cam stepped in, kicked the sword away, and then raised the dagger above the man, poised for a killing blow.

"Cam, no!" Beth yelled. She darted between Cam and the man on the floor. "Don't!"

Cam's eyes snapped up and there was no recognition in them at all, just a crazed need for violence. For one terrifying moment Beth thought he would strike anyway and the knife would find not his attacker's heart, but her own. Her vision went white with fear.

She forced herself to meet his eyes and kept her voice steady. "No. I won't let you do it."

His arm quivered and something like sanity seeped back into his eyes. He stepped back, passed a shaking hand over his face, then sheathed the dagger.

Beth sagged, her legs suddenly like water. She staggered back against the wall.

"Get out! All of ye!" the innkeeper suddenly yelled. "I'll have the sheriff down on ye for this and the laird will hear of it! I willnae have such behaviour in my inn! Get out!"

Cam blinked as though coming out of a deep sleep. His expression twisted and Beth saw anguish in his eyes.

"I...I'm...sorry," he whispered.

He tossed a few coins onto the table and then shouldered his way through the door. The three men he'd downed were beginning to come around, two of them groaning, the third staring into space as though in shock. It was time to leave. Beth pelted up to her room and paused only long enough to grab her bundle of clothes and then hurried out into the yard.

Cam was leading Firefly down the road. She ran to catch up with him.

He glanced at her. "What are ye doing?"

"What's it look like?" she replied, her tone sharp. "I'm coming with you."

He halted. "Ye still want to travel with me? After what happened in there?" His eyes held a haunted look.

"What choice do I have?" she asked. "Those three men will want revenge. If they can't take it out on you, who do you reckon will be next in line?"

He blew out a breath. "Aye, ye are right. I...I shouldnae—"

"Let's just get out of here before they recover and come after us."

They mounted Firefly and left the settlement at a gallop. Beth sat rigid, trying to keep as much distance between herself and Cam as possible. Neither spoke. The silence grew like a wall between them and Beth had no desire to breach it.

They reached a crossroads and Cam took the smallest of the three trails. It looked little used and snaked towards the mountains like a faint ribbon winding through the hilly landscape. Eventually the sun began to fall towards the horizon and still Camdan showed no signs of stopping. Beth though, was tired and her muscles were starting to ache. The long ride and the silence between them was sapping her morale. She wanted nothing more than to curl up by a fire and fall into oblivion.

"We need to find a place to camp," she said. "Before it gets dark."

Up ahead, she spotted a spiky silhouette that stood out against the skyline. As they got closer it resolved itself into a ring of standing stones, tall basalt blocks half-covered in moss and weathered by time that reared out of the earth like jagged teeth.

Seeing it, Cam hissed and jerked Firefly to a halt.

The stones were tall and wide enough that any fire built by their base would be sheltered from the wind. It would make a good place to camp.

"We should stay here," Beth said. "It's about as good a place as I've seen to camp for the night."

Cam didn't reply. Beth looked over her shoulder and found him staring at the ring of stones with a look of fear on his face. Beth started, taken aback.

"What is it? What's wrong?"

"We canna stay here," he whispered. "We have to get away. Now."

He nudged Firefly into a canter, giving the stones a wide berth. His expression was wary and even when they'd passed the circle, he kept looking back over his shoulder until it disappeared in the distance. Beth was puzzled by his reaction but decided not to push it.

Eventually the trail skirted around the edge of a wood. Trees grew close to the trail but didn't encroach, giving a good view of the darkening landscape to the south. The mountains seemed a little nearer and the last rays of the sun illuminated a loch sparkling at their base, looking like an oval mirror reflecting the sky. A few meters from the trail a slight depression formed a kind of grassy bowl that was sheltered from the stiffening breeze.

"We'll camp here," Cam announced.

He pulled Firefly to a halt then swung down from the saddle. He held up a hand to help Beth dismount but she ignored it and struggled down on her own on the other side of the horse, away from him. A quick look of anguish passed across his face, quickly stifled. He pulled off the saddlebags and stalked off.

Beth winced inwardly. She didn't like the thought of causing Camdan pain but after the events in the inn her wariness had come roaring back to the surface. She was painfully aware that she knew next to nothing about him. She found it difficult to reconcile the man who'd come to her rescue in the ravine, the one who'd risked his own life for hers in the clearing, with the cold-blooded, crazed killer that she'd seen at the inn.

She bit her lip and then took off the other saddlebag and carried it into the dell. Cam was crouched in the center, building a fire. In silence Beth knelt and began unpacking. At least Cam had been able to purchase plenty of supplies in the settlement before they'd had to make their quick getaway. In the saddlebag she found two bed rolls, two thick blankets, and the rolled up canvas of a small tent. She shook it out and began erecting it.

Cam glanced her way but didn't comment. Instead, he fetched water from a nearby stream then put the pan on the fire and pulled some provisions from his pack to begin cooking. Soon the smell of frying bacon filled the dell.

Beth shook out the bedrolls and blankets and put them near the fire to warm then sat down cross-legged on her bedroll, staring into the flames. Cam placed the strips of bacon onto freshly buttered bread and handed her one. She nodded her thanks and began eating.

She didn't like the silence between them but she couldn't think of a way to break it. She desperately wanted to talk about the incident this afternoon but Cam's stony silence warned her not to pursue it. Instead, she chose a safer topic.

"This is good," she said around a mouthful of food. "Where did you learn to cook?"

He shrugged. "It's only fried bacon. Any child in Dun Ringill could manage it."

"Dun Ringill? What's that?"

His jaw tightened, as though he'd said more than he intended. "Where I grew up."

"A village?"

He answered reluctantly. "Aye. There is a village that surrounds it but Dun Ringill itself is a castle. The seat of the MacAuley clan."

A castle? He'd grown up in a castle? She glanced at Firefly where he was cropping grass at the edge of the dell. A horse far too grand for a mercenary. Then she looked at the sword that lay by Cam's feet. The hilt was carved with a motif of diving hawks, more expensive than any wandering sell-sword had a right to.

"You're a nobleman aren't you?"

His nostrils flared and the flash of wariness in his eyes told her she'd guessed right.

"Ye ask too many questions."

"And you answer too few of them! You ask about my background but tell me nothing of yours. Where are your family?"

He plucked a blade of grass and began shredding it. He fell silent so long that Beth thought he wouldn't answer.

"My father was Laird David MacAuley," he said at last. "My elder brother was laird after him for a time."

"For a time? You mean he isn't anymore?"

Cam tossed the remnants of the grass into the fire. "Nay. Not anymore." He climbed to his feet. "Finish yer meal. I'm going to have a look around."

He grabbed his sword and stalked off into the night. Beth stared after him. He was a laird's brother. Beth was no expert on Scottish history but she knew that a laird was a lord and a man of some importance. So what was Cam doing out here in the wilds alone? Why was he wandering the Highlands, taking work as a mercenary wherever he could? And why, by Holy God, had he gone berserk in the inn like that?

Stuffing the last bite of her meal into her mouth, Beth scrambled to her feet and followed him. The soft, muddy ground showed Cam's footprints clearly and it wasn't hard to follow his trail. Beth moved carefully through the wood. It was not yet full dark so there was enough light to see by but even so, Beth knew this was probably a stupid move. What if she got lost? Hadn't she learned anything from falling down the ravine? She ought to return to the camp and wait for Cam to come back but she knew she wouldn't. She wanted answers.

From up ahead she heard the 'thunk' of metal on wood and the grunt of physical exertion. Slowly she stalked closer and peered between the branches. Ahead lay a wide clearing that had been created by the fall of a huge oak tree which still lay, half-rotted, across the space. Its bare, dead branches poked into the air like skeletal fingers and the trunk, so wide that Beth was sure it must be at least three times the width of her outstretched arms, took up most of the space.

Camdan was hacking at it.

He'd stripped off his shirt and held his sword. Oblivious to his audience, he whirled and spun and slashed, chopping his blade into the hard wood of the trunk over and over again. Fury rolled off him in waves and even from this distance, Beth could see that look on his face again, that same half-crazed look he'd worn in the inn that afternoon. He moved so fast Beth could hardly keep track of him and a thin sheen of sweat covered his body.

Then Beth's eyes alighted on the tattoo on Cam's arm. The inky black design of interlocking coils was black no longer. Instead it blazed red and angry, like a brand that had been newly pressed into Cam's skin.

Beth's hands flew to her mouth. Holy shit, the pain of such a brand must be unbearable. The sight of it sent a shiver down her spine. She thought suddenly of the ring of standing stones they'd passed and Cam's reaction to them. He'd seemed uneasy, afraid even. Why had he reacted like that? And why was his tattoo glowing? The design of it was similar to the design she'd seen on the walls of the ruins where she'd entered this time. A coincidence?

She shook her head. Everything about him was a mystery. She sensed that being around Camdan MacAuley was dangerous, and not just because of his volatile nature. Secrets swirled around him like smoke.

Careful to make no noise lest Cam notice her spying, she withdrew and returned to camp. She had a lot to think about.

Chapter 8

The rage burned through Cam's veins like fire. As he hacked and slashed at the tree stump, his tattoo, the mark of his terrible bargain, blazed with agony just as it had the night it had been branded into his arm. When it was like this, the urge was so strong he could barely hold on to his sanity. It coursed through his veins like molten metal, demanding violence, demanding blood, and it took all of Cam's strength not to give in, to not become a blood-crazed berserker, killing indiscriminately.

The thought of what would happen if he let it take control was terrifying. Everyone around him would be in danger. *Beth* would be in danger and that was something he could not tolerate. He would die before he let anyone hurt her. Lord above, he would drive his dagger through his own heart before he let *himself* hurt her.

The look in her eyes that afternoon had cut him to the bone. Aye, there had been fear but he was used to that. Nay, it had been the look of utter horror on her face that had sent shame flooding through him like warm tears.

Did she think him a monster? The thought of that was unbearable and, gritting his teeth, he redoubled his attack on the tree stump, taking out his rage and frustration on the old wood, letting it work out of his system.

Curse the Fae! And curse himself for ever agreeing to their bargain!

He shivered suddenly as he remembered the stone circle they'd passed earlier. The sight of it had nearly unmanned him. Over the years he'd avoided all such places. He wanted nothing to do with anything Fae—it had been such a place that had stripped him of his former life and consigned him to this half-life existence.

He swung his arm, the impact of his blade against the wood sending painful shock waves right up into his shoulder. He welcomed the pain. After a while he paused, panting. The tree stump had been hacked viciously, its white inner flesh chopped and gouged into a messy pulp. With a grunt he sheathed his sword. It would need sharpening now he'd used it like an ax.

He glanced at his brand. It was beginning to dull now, returning to the inky black tattoo it appeared to be.

Crossing to the stream he took a quick, cold wash then put his shirt back on before heading back to camp. He spied firelight glimmering through the trees and paused on the edge of the dell.

Beth was sitting cross-legged by the fire. The flames cast a healthy glow onto her features and highlighted the golden strands in her otherwise dark hair. The dress he'd procured fitted her perfectly, accentuating her figure in a way that made Cam's stomach tighten. Lord above, she was captivating. From the crinkle that formed above her nose when she concentrated, to the quick intellect that shone in her deep brown eyes, to the effortless grace of her movements.

Her attention was fixed on something in her lap that Cam couldn't see and from the frown on her face, it was causing her some vexation. She suddenly climbed to her feet and he saw that she was holding a flat rectangular object that was lit up more brightly than any torch. She stretched out her arm, holding the object high and waving it around. After a moment she peered at it, jabbed it with her finger then uttered a curse any sailor would have been proud of.

As Cam watched, perplexed, she began pacing the clearing, holding up the strange object before pressing it to her ear, peering closely at it, then beginning the whole process again. Camdan had never seen the like. What was the lass doing? And what, by all that's holy, was that device?

It was slimmer than the slimmest ledger and would have easily fitted into the palm of Camdan's hand. But it was not a book. What book would glow like that? And was he imagining it or did he see an array of colored icons covering its surface?

"Damn it!" she cried suddenly. "I want to go home! Irene! Just give me a damned cell signal! Is that too much to ask?"

Cam frowned. Secrets. Bethany Carter was surrounded by them.

He stepped into the clearing and she whirled at the sound of his footsteps. She hid the device behind her back and grabbed a stick, holding it up to defend herself.

"Whoa, lass," he said, holding out his hands. "It's only me, dinna go whacking me with that thing."

She breathed out, relaxing slightly. She dropped the stick but didn't bring her arm out from behind her back. "Jeez. You startled me. Has anyone ever told you you move like a cat?"

"Aye, I've heard it said. What is that thing ye are holding?" he asked. "I've never seen aught like it."

She looked a little flustered. "I...um...it's something from home, that's all."

"Aye? Then ye willnae mind me taking a look at it."

She stepped back and raised her chin defiantly. "Actually, I'd rather you didn't."

Annoyance flared in Cam. "Why? Because I might discover something about ye? Because it might tell me who ye really are?"

"I've told you who I am!" she snapped. "Are you calling me a liar?"

"Ye've given me yer name and someplace I've never heard of as yer birthplace. Both of which tell me exactly nothing about who ye are. Ye refuse to answer questions about yer kin. Ye wear jewelry that marks ye out as a noblewoman yet ye clearly know how to set a camp. What am I to make of someone who hides their identity?"

"*Me?* That's rich!" she exploded. "You haven't exactly been forthcoming, have you? You told me you were a mercenary then I find out you're actually the brother of a laird! And the way you reacted to that stone circle was weird in the extreme—like you've been there before or something and you have a tattoo that glows for god's sake! So don't talk to me about hiding!"

Cam went very still. "Ye saw my tattoo glowing? Ye followed me into the woods?"

Uncertainty flashed across her face. "Yes," she mumbled. "But is that any worse than you spying on me?"

"Aye, lass," he breathed, keeping a grip on his anger with an effort. "It is far, far worse. Ye have no idea of what ye could have done."

"So why don't you tell me?" she demanded. "Why don't you tell me what is going on with you?"

His nostrils flared as he struggled to keep his temper. *What should I tell ye?* he thought. *That if ye'd disturbed me whilst in the grip of my rage I might have killed ye? Is that what ye want to hear?*

For one terrible, terrifying instant he almost told her everything. Only his brothers knew the truth of his curse and they were both lost to him as surely as if they'd died that night on the beach. How good it would feel for somebody else to know the truth, to stop pretending and let his mask slip, if only for a moment.

But he snapped his mouth shut. He couldn't tell her. Long years of hiding who he was had become too ingrained for him to break the habit now. Besides, if she knew the truth she would run from him in horror and she would be right to do so.

"There's naught to tell," he snapped. "Naught that ye would understand."

"That's a poor evasion," she said, crossing her arms and glaring at him.

"Is that so?" he snapped back. "Easier than diverting attention so ye dinna have to answer *my* questions? Do ye think I'm stupid, woman? Do ye think I havenae noticed how ye still havenae answered anything I've asked ye?"

She glared at him for a moment before stomping off towards the fire where she promptly disappeared inside the tent. Cam stared after her. Lord above, but the lass could be infuriating! Infuriating and intriguing at the same time. What was he to do with her?

With a growl of annoyance he made his way to his own sleeping mat and rolled up in his cloak. For a long time he lay there with eyes open, staring into the fire as full dark settled around them. What was he going to do about Bethany Carter?

BETH WOKE SLOWLY THE next morning, rousing gradually from strange dreams of standing stones and roaring waves. She opened bleary eyes and found herself staring up at undyed canvas. She'd slept soundly but didn't feel refreshed and had a nagging unease in the back of her mind as though she'd been having nightmares she couldn't quite remember.

Scrubbing at grainy eyes with the heels of her hands, she sat up and yawned. From the light seeping in from the badly tied tent flap, she knew it was after dawn.

She wondered how Cam had fared last night sleeping outside and felt a little twinge of guilt. Their argument had left her unsettled and edgy. She'd been terrified when he saw her with her cell phone and had cursed herself for her stupidity. Why had she taken it out? Did she *want* him to know she was a time-traveler?

Um, no. Definitely not. Camdan's unpredictable moods meant there was no way to know how he'd react to that little revelation.

Besides, she thought. *I only got the cell out because he freaked me out so much yesterday. That fight at the inn and then him attacking that log. He frightened me. Was it any wonder I needed some connection with home?*

Her rationalization did nothing to assuage her guilt. She didn't like lying to him even though she knew she had no choice.

She pulled in a deep breath, stretched her arms over her head and then slowly moved her head from side to side to work out the stiffness. Moving to the tent flap, she yanked it open and stepped outside. The dawn air was cold enough to send goose bumps riding across her skin and she wrapped her arms around herself to keep warm. Lazy streamers of mist lay close to the ground and wove around the tree trunks like wispy gauze.

There was no sign of Camdan.

She spun around, searching the clearing. His bedroll was gone and there was no sign of his pack. She felt a twinge of panic. Where the hell was he? Had he abandoned her because of one little argument?

A noise from behind sent her spinning in that direction. Firefly's long nose poked out of a bush as he ripped leaves from it and munched noisily. Beth let out a sigh of relief. If Firefly was here it meant Camdan could not be far.

She crossed the clearing to where Firefly was busy with his breakfast. The horse swung his head up as she approached and snorted in greeting.

"Where's your master, eh?" she said.

Firefly sniffed at her outstretched hand and then went back to eating. She patted him on the neck.

"You're not so scary really, are you? Not once I've gotten to know you. I reckon your master's a bit like that too. Don't you?"

Leaving the horse to his meal, she fetched water from the stream and had a quick wash. The water was icy enough to make her gasp and she got it over with as quickly as possible. She split the end of a twig and used it as a rudimentary toothbrush then pulled her fingers through her hair to take out the worst of the tangles. She must look a state. Oh, what she wouldn't give for a decent hairbrush and a pair of straighteners!

Having made herself as presentable as she could, she pulled her bedroll from inside the tent and placed it by the fire, sat cross-legged on it and began coaxing the fire into life.

A branch snapped and Beth looked up to see Cam striding through the mist into the dell. His red-gold hair shone with droplets of dew and his cheeks held a warm glow as though he'd been running. In one hand he held a bow and from the other dangled a pair of pheasants.

Relief flooded through her at the sight of him. The dell seemed suddenly warmer, more welcoming with him in it, and the faint anxiety gnawing at her stomach evaporated.

She scrambled to her feet and raised an eyebrow at him, folding her arms across her chest. "And where, pray tell, have you been?" She kept her voice playful, trying to tell him she wanted to put last night's argument behind them.

"Finding our supper for later," he replied, brandishing the pheasants. "See?"

She screwed up her face and stepped back. "Lovely." She eyed the bow. "So I can add hunting to your long list of talents?"

He shrugged. "With the bow I am average at best. My younger brother was always the best marksman in the clan."

Cam's tattoo, she noticed, had faded to a dull gray, hardly noticeable at all against his skin. She frowned. How the hell could a tattoo keep changing color? It made no sense.

"Well, since you've caught supper I reckon it's only fair that I cook breakfast, don't you?"

He dropped the pheasants to the ground and then seated himself by the fire. "Ye'll get no argument from me on that score, lass. I'm beginning to understand that arguing with ye is a futile business."

"Ah! You're learning. I knew there was hope for you yet."

He gave her a small smile and Beth's heart fluttered. She hoped their argument last night was forgotten.

The way he was sitting made his plaid ride up his legs. Above the soft leather boots that reached to his knees, Beth caught a glimpse of his knee and a muscled thigh. She swallowed.

"Right. Coming up."

She turned to the saddlebags and began rummaging inside, coming out with some sausages which she tumbled into the pan. They sizzled as they hit the metal, frying in their own juices and sending a delicious scent through the dell. She tossed in some field mushrooms as well and then crouched beside the fire, moving the sausages around the pan with a wooden spatula.

Camdan watched her while she worked. Beth forced herself to concentrate on her task. She was glad when the sausages were cooked and she doled out Cam's share onto a small wooden plate. He nodded his thanks and began eating.

Beth sat back and tucked into her own breakfast. They ate quickly then Cam announced it was time to be going. Together they broke camp, Cam dousing the fire and packing away the tent whilst Beth washed the cooking equipment in the stream and then packed up the supplies. They worked without speaking, neither having to give the other instruction, moving in concert as if they'd done this together countless times.

Less than an hour after waking Beth found herself sitting in the saddle in front of Cam as they swung back onto the trail that led higher into the mountains.

"Where are we heading?" she asked. "Wouldn't we be better keeping to a main road?"

"Only if ye want to go out of yer way by many days," he replied. "Edinburgh lies beyond the mountains and the quickest route cuts through them. Dinna worry, lass. The passes will still be open. Winter has yet to bite so we'll be fine. Besides, I have other reasons for wanting to pass this way."

She craned her neck to look at him and found he had a mischievous smile on his face. "Reasons you're not going to tell me, I'm guessing."

"Ye guessed right. Dinna look at me like that! Ye'll be glad we came this way, I promise ye."

Beth gave him a scowl. Him and his damned secrets!

The day was fine and bright with wisps of cloud scudding along high above. The leaves shimmered golden and red in the sunlight and the rustle of squirrels hiding acorns in the leaf litter accompanied the clop of Firefly's hooves. Beth soon found herself drowsing in the saddle.

The faint echo of Irene MacAskill's words sounded in her head, like a dream that fades on waking. *Yer destiny is coming for ye, Bethany Carter. What will ye do? Will ye run? Or will ye face it?*

She paid the memory no heed. Right now she was warm and comfortable and was leaning against something reassuringly strong. She felt safe, safer than she had in a long time.

What need did she have to fear the ramblings of some mad old woman?

Blinking, she tried to clear her foggy thoughts. That reassuring warmth at her back was still there and she realized she was leaning against Cam. A weight across her body was his arm holding her against him. She sprang bolt upright with a gasp and Cam released his grip.

"Ye fell asleep, lass," he said by way of explanation. "I held ye to ensure ye didnae fall from the saddle, that's all."

His voice was wary. Did he think he'd scared her? It wasn't fear that made Beth's skin tingle from their contact. But she couldn't tell him that.

"Right. Thanks," Beth mumbled, flustered.

Cam stiffened suddenly behind her. "Hush."

Beth froze. Cam reached slowly over his shoulder and gripped the hilt of his sword.

"I wouldnae do that if I were ye," said a voice from behind them. "I have an arrow trained on ye. Take yer hand away from yer blade or I will make a pincushion out of ye."

With a low growl that rumbled through his chest, Cam slowly took his hand from his sword hilt. "Ye will regret threatening me, little man, when I find out who ye are."

There was a long pause. "I know that voice. Cam? Is that ye?"

Beth heard rustling in the undergrowth and a man stepped into their path. A hunting bow dangled from one hand.

"Rabbie?" Cam said incredulously. He barked a sudden laugh. "Burn me, but I should have known it was ye! Ye are the only man in all of Alba who can creep up on me unawares!"

He swung his leg over the saddle and dropped to the ground. The two men came together in a warm embrace, grinning and slapping each other on the back.

"Ah, but it's good to see ye, my old friend," Cam said. "I didnae expect to find ye this far down the trail. Tis a good long ways yet to yer place."

"Aye," Rabbie replied. "And Elspeth will spit feathers when she knows I've been down here again but there have been signs of mounted men passing through here and I was checking out their trail."

Cam shook his head. "We've come up from Netherlay and saw nay sign of anyone on the trail up here."

Rabbie nodded. "I hope ye are right." His eyes flicked to Beth and a curious expression flitted across his ruddy features.

Cam cleared his throat. "Rabbie, this is Bethany Carter, a traveler from across the sea. I'm escorting her to Edinburgh. Beth, I would like ye to meet my good friend, Rabbie MacGovern."

Beth swung her leg over the saddle and slid awkwardly to the ground. She wiped her palms down her dress and held out her hand. "Pleased to meet you, Rabbie."

Rabbie looked a little taken aback then he took her hand and shook it. "Likewise, Bethany Carter. I canna begin to imagine what calamity caused ye to take Camdan MacAuley as a traveling companion. The man complains worse than a fishwife."

Beth laughed. "Yes and has a temper like an angry bear."

"Aye, one that's stood on a thorn."

Cam crossed his arms. "Have ye two finished? Rabbie, could I beg yer hospitality for a day or so?"

"Cam, my old friend," Rabbie said, clapping him on the shoulder. "Ye dinna have to beg anything. Elspeth would strip my hide if I didnae insist on ye staying with us. Come on. If we hurry we can be home in time for supper."

The woodsman led the way and Cam grabbed Firefly's reins as the three of them began walking north along the trail. It felt good to walk after two days in the saddle. Beth's thighs and backside were aching something rotten.

Rabbie proved to be talkative and friendly. He made polite enquires about Beth's background and she answered as best she could without giving away too much information. He accepted her answers with a nod and didn't push for explanations, for which she was grateful.

He explained that he and his family lived not far away in an isolated cottage. Rabbie made his living by hunting and trapping, selling his wares twice a year in the market at Aberdeen. Beth wondered how he and Cam knew each other. From their friendly banter it was obvious they liked and respected each other. In looks they couldn't be more different. One walked with the casual grace of a born warrior, weapons strapped around his person. The other carried only a bow and wore the simple garments of a woodsman, his ruddy face testament to many long days spent out in the elements. Yet they both radiated self-reliance earned through hard toil.

"Ah! Home, at last!" Rabbie announced.

Up ahead smoke was rising in a dark column above the treeline. The trail veered around an outcropping of rock and came out onto a wide plateau below a sheer cliff-face. Nestled against the cliff, Beth spied a neat and tidy thatched cottage. The flat ground in front of it formed a barnyard complete with fenced enclosures that held two goats and a milk-cow. Beyond the cottage lay a chicken-house and a small barn. Strangely, the cottage had a wooden ramp leading up to the door.

The cottage door opened and a small red-haired woman stepped out. The arms of her dress were rolled up to her elbows and a dusting of flour on her nose showed she'd been disturbed in her baking.

Rabbie's face broke into a grin. "Wife!" he called. "I hope ye've made plenty of bannocks! We have guests!"

The woman's eyes fell on Cam and widened. "Camdan MacAuley! As I live and breathe!"

Cam's grin was every bit as wide as Rabbie's. "Ah, Elspeth, ye look more beautiful than I remember!"

"Get away with ye and yer silver tongue!" Elspeth said. "And come here, ye big lump."

She pulled Cam into a tight embrace and then pushed him to arm's length, looking him over critically. "Ye seem...well," she said carefully. "Are ye?"

Cam glanced at Beth. "Aye," he muttered. "For the most part. Elspeth, there's someone here I'd like ye to meet."

He quickly introduced Beth and explained the circumstances of their meeting. Elspeth greeted Beth as warmly as her husband had. She ignored Beth's proffered hand and pulled her into a hug instead.

"I'm delighted to meet ye, my dear! An outlander? I'm sure ye have lots of interesting tales to tell. Ye can tell us some round the fire tonight!"

"I...um...okay," Beth stammered, swept along by Elspeth's enthusiasm. "But there's not much to tell really."

"Not much to tell?" Elspeth exclaimed. "An outlander from over the sea helps our Cam against bandits and ye reckon there's naught to tell? Pah! Nay doubt ye've seen much of the world. Ah, how I would love to travel! France! Italy!"

"Wife," Rabbie said, raising an eyebrow. "Ye dinna even like going into Aberdeen. Ye reckon the noise and bustle gives ye hives!"

"Aye," Elspeth said with a smile. "But that doesnae mean I canna dream, does it? Come on," she said to Cam. "I know someone who'll be mighty excited ye've returned to us."

She turned and led the way towards the cottage. "Travis!" she yelled. "Look who's here to see ye!"

The squeak of trundling wheels came from inside the cottage and a seated figure emerged into the light. Beth startled in surprise. The young boy was around eight—and he was in a wheelchair. It was a rudimentary design made from wood. The wheels on either side looked like they might once have belonged on a small cart and two smaller wheels on pivots would allow the chair to change direction. A raised rim around the wheel hub allowed the boy to grip as he turned the wheels, moving himself expertly onto the veranda. The ramp in front of the house suddenly made perfect sense.

"Uncle Cam!" the boy shouted in delight.

"Travis, ye young whipper snapper!" Cam cried. He ran over, took the boy by the waist, and lifted him effortlessly from the chair. He spun him around—making the boy squeal with delight—before settling him atop his shoulders. "I hope ye've been behaving yerself for yer ma and da".

The boy nodded enthusiastically. "I've been verra good, havenae I, Ma?"

"Well, that depends on yer meaning of 'good' doesnae it, Travis, my boy?" Elspeth replied. "I see ye havenae finished yer tasks yet. The chickens still need feeding."

"But Ma!" the boy wailed. "I want to talk to Uncle Cam!"

"And ye will, when ye've done what I've asked of ye," Elspeth said firmly.

"That sounds fair to me, little man," Cam rumbled. "Why dinna ye go and see to those chickens then come inside? But before ye do, there's someone I'd like ye to meet. This is my friend, Beth. She's come all the way from Edinburgh to see us."

Travis turned to look at Beth, his eyes going round with curiosity.

Beth smiled at him. "Hi. Nice to meet you, Travis."

Travis gazed up at her, suddenly shy.

"Wow, would you look at that?" Beth said. "That's a mighty fine tunic you're wearing, Travis. What a handsome boy you are!"

The compliment had the desired affect. Travis beamed. "Ma made it for me. The wool came from our sheep, Molly. Would ye like to meet her?"

"I would!" Beth laughed. "Maybe you could introduce us later, when you've done your chores?"

He nodded.

Cam lowered him back into his chair and Travis set his hands to the wheels and pushed himself down the ramp and onto one of the well-worn paths that led around the farm. The path was made of smooth, compacted earth and Beth realized Rabbie and Elspeth must have worked the paths deliberately, compacting them until they were smooth enough for their son to be able to get around their little farm in his chair.

Beth looked at the crofters with new admiration. Scraping a living out here in this unforgiving wilderness must be hard enough, but to do so whilst caring for a disabled child took a dedication and determination that Beth found inspiring.

She followed them to the door but paused on the threshold. She looked back, watching Travis. Shouldn't somebody stay to supervise the child? But as she watched, she realized there was no need. Everything had been made to suit his needs. The latches on the chicken run were low enough for him to reach, the gate wide enough for him to wheel his chair through. She heard him talking to the chickens and as he went inside the birds flocked around him, eager for their dinner. The boy worked with easy self-sufficiency. Beth smiled to herself. Something about the sight of Travis lifted her spirits. It spoke to her of hope.

She followed the others into the cottage. The first thing she noticed was that it was far bigger than it appeared from the outside. There were several rooms off a central hallway and the place was neat and tidy—far more comfortable than she'd expected from a lonely croft in the mountains. The walls were thick and appeared to be made of cob—a mixture of mud and straw that hardened like concrete—and had been smoothed with lime plaster. The floor was constructed of flat stones that looked like they might have come from a river bed and thick wooden beams framed the doorways and held up the roof. She felt another of her preconceptions evaporate. This was no peasant's hut but a snug, well-crafted home.

Elspeth ushered them into the main room where a large fireplace dominated one wall. Sides of meat hung from hooks and a bread oven built into the side was giving off a delicious smell. A trestle table set before the fire was still strewn with flour and dough.

"Would ye look at that?" Elspeth tutted. "Such a mess! And in front of guests!"

She quickly swept the table clean and then dragged it to one side out of the way. In its place she put four wooden chairs in a semi-circle around the fire and bade them all to sit. Beth took a seat next to Cam and sighed gratefully as she sat back, stretching her feet towards the fire.

Rabbie took out a flask and poured whisky into small, pottery cups. Beth nodded her thanks as she accepted hers, cupping the tiny beaker in both hands and inhaling the heady aroma of the spirit.

"A toast," Rabbie said, holding up his cup. "To the return of old friends and meeting new ones."

Beth raised her glass then downed the whisky in one. She knew what to expect this time but the fiery liquid still sent her into a fit of coughing. She leaned forward and Cam thumped her on the back.

"Wow," she muttered when the coughing fit had passed. "I think that just about blew my head off."

Rabbie laughed. "Would ye like another? There's plenty more where that came from."

Beth waved her hand. "Whilst I appreciate the offer I prefer to keep my head on my shoulders."

Elspeth nodded sagely. "Most wise, my dear. Rabbie would bathe in whisky if he could. He thinks it's the only liquid in all the Highlands."

Rabbie gave his wife a quizzical look. "Ye mean there are others?"

Elspeth raised an eyebrow but didn't deign to respond. "Right. Now that Travis is busy mayhap ye can tell us what brings ye up this way, Cam. And why Beth is traveling with ye."

Beth shared a glanced with Cam. He nodded.

"I...um...I came out here from Edinburgh," she began hesitantly. "But I lost my guide. I stumbled on Cam in the woods near Cannoch and he offered to guide me home."

Rabbie frowned. "My, that is a long way. It will take ye many days to get there."

"Which is why we came this way," Cam said. "The passes through the mountains will cut the length of the journey."

"Aye, that it will," Rabbie said thoughtfully. "But ye will need to be careful. Ye remember I said there were groups of mounted men roaming the lower trails? Well, there's rumors they're MacGregor's men and that he's holed up round here somewhere after being chased out of his last hideout by the laird. If that's so then ye need to be careful. He wasnae best pleased with what ye did to him, Cam."

Cam's expression turned stony. "I am nay afraid of MacGregor, although I reckon yer worries are unfounded. His base was in the north west. He wouldnae come this far east."

"Mayhap he wouldnae, given the choice. But he wasnae given any choice if the rumors are correct. The MacAuleys and the MacConnells launched a joint force to drive the brigands from their borders. MacGregor was lucky to escape with his life by all accounts. The MacAuleys have a new laird and he gave MacGregor and his men a sound thrashing before they were able to retreat."

Cam's head came up suddenly. "There's a new laird in Dun Ringill?"

"Aye," Rabbie said, rubbing his chin. "Goes by the name of Logan. Logan MacAuley."

The blood drained from Cam's face and he went deathly pale. He stood abruptly. "I...I...must see to Firefly."

Without another word he hurried out the door. Beth stood to follow him but Elspeth caught her arm. "Best to let him go, my dear. These moods come on him sometimes and we've learned its best to leave him be when he does. Ye must be tired after yer long journey. Here, come with me."

Beth glanced out into the yard. She could see Cam taking off Firefly's saddle. His movements were jerky and tense and she knew him well enough by now to read unease in his stance. She sighed. He probably would not welcome her company right now.

Turning away, she followed Elspeth across the hallway and into one of the other rooms of the house. A narrow bed lay along one wall with a dressing table and mirror against the other.

Beth stared. Oh god! A mirror! And, was she imagining things, or was that a hairbrush?

Elspeth noticed her staring and laughed. "We sometimes get trader caravans coming through here in the summer. They keep us supplied with what we canna provide for ourselves, including a few little luxuries. Here, sit down and I'll brush yer hair."

Beth did as she was bid, perching on the little stool by the dressing table. "You've been very kind," Beth observed. "Thank you."

Elspeth waved away the thanks and then picked up the hairbrush. "Nonsense. To be honest, tis good to have another woman around and any friend of Cam's is a friend of mine."

"You seem to know him pretty well."

She laughed at that. "Aye, we do. About as well as anyone can know Camdan MacAuley. That lad is better at keeping secrets than any confessor priest, I can tell ye."

Beth smiled. "Ah, so you've noticed that?"

"Let's just say I've learned when to pry and when to leave him be. Now, lean forward a little."

Elspeth began brushing Beth's hair as though she was some grand lady. It seemed strange being pampered like this but Beth didn't make any complaint. It felt wonderful. Elspeth was careful not to snag her hair and the gentle tugs on her scalp eased away her worries better than any massage.

"You're good at this," Beth murmured. "You should get a job as a masseuse. Any posh spa would be glad to have you."

"I'm sure I dinna know what those words are!" Elspeth laughed. "But I'll take it as a compliment." She cocked her head in the mirror as she regarded Beth. "Yer accent isnae one I recognize. Are ye Spanish? French?"

"Neither," Beth replied. "I'm American."

Elspeth frowned. "I canna say as I've heard of such a place. It must be a very long way away. Ye must miss it terribly."

Beth thought about this and was surprised to find that she didn't miss home half as much as she thought she would. Sure, she missed her friends. She missed modern comforts like hot showers and a comfy mattress. But beyond that? There was nothing pulling her back, nothing that anchored her to the twenty-first century. She had no family. Not anymore.

She shrugged, uncomfortable with Elspeth's scrutiny. "Yeah, I guess. And work are probably going crazy by now trying to cover my shifts."

"Work?" Elspeth asked. "Ye work in yer homeland?"

"Yes. In a coffee shop. Although I'm training to be a human rights lawyer."

Elspeth's eyes widened. "A lawyer? The only lawyers I know of reside in the king's court and have studied in the great Italian universities. Surely only men can aspire to such a calling?"

"Not where I'm from," Beth answered with a laugh. "Anyone can do it. Although finding a damned placement isn't easy." She looked at Elspeth. "What about you?"

"Naught so grand. I grew up in a village on the banks of Loch Tay. My father was a fisherman and my brothers and I used to help out on the boats when I was a girl. I thought I'd marry a fisherman and my children would go into the trade after their father. That all changed one day when a trapper by the name of Rabbie MacGovern came to my village to sell his pelts."

"So he swept you off your feet?"

"Aye, something like that." She paused in her brushing, eyes going wistful. "He was the most handsome man I'd ever seen. I still remember the first time I saw him. I felt like my heart had stopped. He asked me to dance that night at the summer fair and within the week he'd asked my father's permission to marry me." She shrugged. "So here I am."

Beth felt something shift inside her. Elspeth radiated contentment in a way she herself had never experienced. She and Rabbie had built a life for themselves out here and it was more than enough for Elspeth.

Beth was suddenly struck by the differences between her own time and this one. In the twenty-first century life was lived at breakneck speed. Everyone was always striving, always yearning for something more. There was always the latest gadget to buy, the latest fashion to follow, the latest gossip to catch up on. But here? Here there was only the now and the simple pleasure of enjoying what you had.

Beth had never thought about it like that before and the sudden insight left her a little unsettled. The twenty-first century was her home. It was where she belonged. Wasn't it?

"Are ye all right?" Elspeth asked.

Beth shook herself. "I'm fine. I was just thinking about how happy you and Rabbie seem. And your house is wonderful."

Elspeth smiled warmly at the compliment. "That's mighty kind of ye to say so. Rabbie built it. He has a knack for building things. And Cam helped, of course. The two of them worked night and day for months to give us this."

Cam? Beth thought. *He helped build the house?*

"How do you know him?" Beth asked.

"Through happy accident," Elspeth replied. "Or unhappy maybe, considering the circumstances of our meeting." She pursed her lips, her eyes becoming thoughtful. "It was several years ago now. Rabbie was out setting his traps on the upper trails when he came across a body lying by the side of the trail with a warhorse cropping the grass nearby. Except it wasnae a body, it was Cam, filthy, starved and on the cusp of death. Rabbie brought him here and I nursed him back to health. It was a long road and more than once we thought he wouldnae make it, despite our best efforts. We didnae know what had befallen him but it was obvious he'd been in a battle. He was covered in wounds and there was a hole right through his thigh that could only have been made with the point of a spear. It was a miracle he'd survived as long as he had alone on the mountain trails."

"Did he tell you what happened?"

Elspeth shook her head. "He never talked about it and we didnae ask. People come up into these mountains to escape from something. Eventually he recovered and he stayed with us for around six months. Helped Rabbie build this place. Built the wheelchair for Travis. Every so often a black mood would come on him and he would disappear for a day or so. When he came back he seemed a little better. Then, when he was finally healed, he left. Said he couldn't live on our charity forever. We were sad to see him go. Having him around the place was a great help and Travis adores him. But he comes back every now and then, bringing us things he thinks we might need."

Beth remained silent, mulling over Elspeth's words. Just when she thought she'd got Cam figured out she discovered something about him that threw everything into a muddle again. The fact he'd been injured in a battle didn't surprise her. The fact that he'd designed and built Travis's wheelchair did.

If she had any sense at all she ought to distance herself from Camdan MacAuley. He was dangerous. Any sensible person would steer well clear. But she was no longer sensible where he was concerned. Damn it! What was happening to her?

"There," Elspeth said, stepping back. "All done."

Beth looked at herself in the mirror. The snarls had been worked free and now her hair spilled over her shoulders like a shiny blanket. She grinned at Elspeth.

"Wow. Who's that in the mirror? I'm sure I don't recognize her."

Elspeth snorted a laugh and moved over to a trunk. She pulled out some clothes which she laid on the bed and then poured water into a large bowl.

"There's some soap on the dressing table. I make it myself from lavender that grows further down the valley. I'll leave ye to have a wash and I've taken the liberty of laying out some fresh clothing. Ye look around the same size as me so I reckon some of my old dresses should fit ye. Help yerself to whatever ye need."

Beth scraped the stool back and stood. She caught Elspeth's hands in both her own. "I don't know how I can repay your kindness."

Elspeth blushed. "Dinna be daft," she said. "What are friends for?"

Beth smiled. Friends. She liked the sound of that.

"I'll be in the other room trying to get that unruly son of mine to practise his letters," Elspeth said. "Take yer time and join us when ye are ready."

After she'd left Beth washed and then changed. As she dressed she thought about what Elspeth had told her of Cam's background. Where had he come from? And what battle had he been involved in?

The only thing she'd managed to glean from him was that he was the brother of a former laird. As his name was MacAuley, it followed that his brother must have been Laird MacAuley. Hmm. Beth's eyes narrowed in thought. Rabbie had told them that the MacAuleys had a new laird—a guy called Logan—and Cam's reaction to the name had been instantaneous. Beth frowned. The name obviously meant something to him.

Beth shifted uncomfortably. There was something going on here. Something she didn't understand. She got the feeling she was in way over her head, that there were currents and plots swirling around her of which she was woefully ignorant.

It all started with Irene MacAskill, Beth thought. *Could this all be connected? Could my tumble back in time, my meeting with Cam, his hidden past and the tattoo on his arm all lead back to one old woman?*

Her eyebrows pulled together as she thought back to the words Irene had spoken to her before she'd stepped through the arch. *Ye are running, my dear. Running from the past, thinking that if ye can only become a lawyer ye can somehow fix the wrongs that were done to ye. But it doesnae work that way. Ye canna find happiness by running from yer past: only by running towards yer future. Are ye ready to do that, Bethany Carter? Are ye ready to find yer true path?*

What had Irene meant by that? She wasn't running from her past! How ridiculous! True, she'd left the US and all the painful memories it held but she'd come to Edinburgh to study. It didn't mean she'd been running away. It didn't!

Beth closed her eyes and thought back to that January day. Even now her thoughts shied away from it as though it was an old wound that would reopen if she pressed it. But she forced herself to remember. She remembered the knock on the door. She remembered opening it. She remembered the sight of the police car parked on the street. She remembered the sombre expressions of the two officers standing on her doorstep. She remembered...

No! she thought. *That has nothing to do with any of this! Nothing!*

But she was no longer so sure. Did her own past and her destiny have something to do with Cam? Was he the reason Irene had brought her here?

She blew out a breath and placed her hands on her hips, thinking. Since the moment she'd got here she'd been swept away by events out of her control. It was time to take back that control. Starting with some answers.

She went into the main room where she found Elspeth sitting at the table with Travis. From outside came the sound of Rabbie splitting wood. There was no sign of Cam. Travis was holding a piece of chalk in his fingers and peering at a slate tablet. He looked up when Beth walked in.

"Beth!" he said. "Would ye like a game of cat's cradle?"

"Nay, young man," Elspeth scolded. "No more games until ye have finished yer letters. Uncle Cam will take a look when he comes back. Ye wouldnae want to disappoint him would ye?"

The stricken look on Travis's face answered that question. Beth smiled and ruffled Travis's hair. "We'll have a game later, promise." She turned to look at Elspeth. "Do you know where Cam is?"

"He hasnae come back yet. He'll either be in the barn seeing to his horse or down by the lake." She nodded in the direction of the northern trail. "About ten minutes walk that way."

Beth nodded her thanks and set off to find him.

Chapter 9

Despite the cool Highland evening, Cam's body gleamed with sweat and his lungs were burning. Good. That's what he wanted. He'd come out here to practise his sword forms and also to forget. He moved effortlessly into the next form, the sword blade singing through the air, glittering like a bar of silver in the gathering dusk before holding the pose until his biceps quivered.

Several paces away lay the edge of Loch Morn. It wasn't big enough to be a loch really, just a mountain lake, but to Camdan it was one of the most beautiful places in the Highlands. Perfectly circular, the lake was so smooth and still that it reflected the sky above in perfect detail until it was hard to tell where sky ended and land began.

He'd come to this spot often whilst he'd been recovering with Rabbie and Elspeth. It was here, sitting on this bank in the lonely wilds of the Highlands, that Camdan had begun to piece his life back together, such as it was.

His arm muscles quivered as he held another pose and the sword-tip dropped. He grunted in annoyance and raised it, forcing his rebellious muscles to obey. His father had taught he and his brothers the sword forms long ago and insisted they practise every morning.

When Camdan had taken over as commander of the Dun Ringill garrison, he'd impressed the same discipline on his men. Even on dark, cold winter mornings, he and his warriors would be out in the bailey going through the forms. Sometimes his elder brother would join them when his duties as laird allowed, and even more rarely, his younger brother, Finlay. But Finn was not a born soldier and more often than not he would miraculously disappear when it was time for sword practice and then miraculously reappear again just in time for breakfast.

Camdan smiled at the memory and then glanced down at the tattoo on his forearm. It was not glowing. In fact, it had faded to a light gray and his rage lay quiet, quieter than it had in months.

Being here helped, of course. It was the place where he'd started to calm the turmoil in his soul, to forge a new life out of the wreckage of the old. Being near Elspeth, Rabbie and little Travis was like a balm. They were his dearest friends, as close as family, and it warmed his heart to visit with them again.

And then there was Bethany Carter.

He stumbled as he thought of her, losing the form. He frowned at himself and swiped the air with his blade, regaining the pose.

Bethany Carter.

Her face flashed into his mind and it was all he could do to keep concentration. That smile. Those eyes. That fierce, brave intelligence.

Aye, being near her helped as well.

He knew he ought to keep her at arm's length and avoid any kind of attachment but the more time he spent with her the more time he *wanted* to spend with her. He found himself looking for her when he walked into a room and dreaming about her when he was wrapped in his cloak alone at night.

Resolutely, he pushed thoughts of her from his mind and instead thought of what Rabbie had told him earlier. *The MacAuleys have a new laird. Goes by the name of Logan. Logan MacAuley.*

Cam shook his head, flinging sweat from his hair. Logan could not be laird. It was impossible. The bargain they'd made ensured that.

He fell still, the sword clasped loosely. A heron was wading slowly through the reeds at the lake's edge, eyes fixed on the still water as it searched for fish. A gentle breeze swept through the leaves, making them whisper.

He heard a footstep and whirled, bringing his sword around in a glittering arc. Before he realized what he was doing, he'd placed the tip against Beth's throat, who was standing two paces behind him.

Her eyes went wide and her lips parted in a gasp. Camdan snatched the blade away and sheathed it.

"Are ye mad?" he snapped at her. "Why did ye sneak up on me like that? I could have skewered ye!"

Beth massaged the base of her throat where the blade had rested. "I wasn't sneaking anywhere," she replied indignantly, her eyes flashing with annoyance. "I made plenty of noise and shouted you more than once."

She had? He hadn't heard a thing. Cam ran a hand through his hair. "Aye, well," he mumbled. "I was a little...distracted."

Beth's gaze flicked over the myriad of white-scars that criss-crossed his body and then came to rest on his tattoo. A look he couldn't decipher crossed her face. Disgust? Pity? He snatched up his shirt and yanked it over his head.

"What do ye want?" he demanded.

"I came to see if you're okay."

"I'm fine. Why wouldnae I be?"

She took a step closer. The setting sun made her eyes shine. "You seemed a little...ruffled earlier, when Rabbie mentioned the MacAuley clan—your clan— having a new laird. And then you didn't come back after stabling Firefly. Are you sure you're okay?"

The concern in her eyes made his annoyance drain away. He suddenly couldn't bear the compassion in her gaze. He whirled and stalked down to the water's edge, gazing out over the placid waters. She didn't say anything or come any closer but he felt her presence standing behind him. If he closed his eyes, he was sure he could pinpoint her exact position. Lord above, when had he become so attuned to her?

He wished she would leave. He wished she would come closer and press her hands against his back. He wished...curse it, he didn't know what he wished.

The silence stretched, broken only by the raucous cry of a pheasant somewhere in the underbrush.

"Elspeth told me how Rabbie found you," Beth said at last. "And how they nursed you back to health."

Cam clenched his fists. "She shouldnae have done that."

"Why?" Beth cried, her tone annoyed now. "Another one of your secrets?"

He frowned at her. "This conversation is over."

She threw up her hands in exasperation. "Damn it, Camdan! Why do you block me at every turn? Why don't you trust me?"

He opened his mouth and shut it again. Trust her? He didn't trust anyone. He dare not. "Ye dinna understand," he said. "Everything I do, I do to keep ye safe."

"Keep me safe? From who?"

He met her angry gaze. "From me."

She looked taken aback. "You would never hurt me," she asserted. "I trust you."

Now it was Cam's turn to be surprised. She trusted him? After what he'd done at the inn? Lord, he wished he trusted himself.

"Ye dinna understand, lass."

"No, you're right there. So help me understand. Why are you like two different people?"

"I dinna ken what ye mean."

"Don't you?" she replied. "What I'm struggling to get my head around is the difference between the man who fought those thugs at the inn and the man I see before me now. The man at the inn was off his head, out of control. I think you would have killed that guy if I hadn't stopped you. But the man standing in front of me right now is the man who built a wheelchair for a disabled kid, helped a family build their home, risked his life to save a stranger from a gang of criminals and then volunteered to escort that stranger halfway across the country. It's that man who freaked out when we passed a stone circle, that man who was brother to the laird of the MacAuley. Which man are you really, Cam?"

"Both," he replied in a hoarse whisper. "One is the man that lurks inside me, the other is the one I strive to be."

He turned to look out over the stillness of the lake for a moment, yearning for a peace that had fled. He churned inside. He turned back to Beth.

"Dinna ask me to explain. Ye would hate me if ye knew the truth."

BETH'S HEART TWISTED as Cam turned to look at her. The expression on his face was ravaged. She read self-revulsion, fear, and a deep, aching vulnerability.

She bit her lip and struggled to think of what to say. What could she say that would get through? Tell him that she wouldn't hate him if she knew the truth? He wouldn't believe her. For the first time since she met him, Cam's emotions were written clearly to see, the brittle inner core of him exposed. It made her want to run to him. It made her want to wrap her arms around him and pull him close.

But she didn't. She suspected such a move would snap his self-restraint. What the hell had happened to him to cause such deep and abiding self-loathing? She'd asked him to trust her but now, as she looked at the shadows that lurked behind his eyes, she realized that Cam trusted nobody and had not done so for a very, very long time.

You can trust me! she wanted to shout. *Don't you realize that yet?*

As they stood facing each other, the sun setting behind the lake and the silence growing between them like a wall, a sudden realization came to Beth.

Trust went both ways.

Tell him, a voice whispered in the back of her mind. *Tell him the truth.*

The thought scared her. It would leave her dangerously vulnerable. She blew out a breath and then rubbed at her eyes, trying to gather her courage.

"It's time for some honesty between us," she said, lifting her chin. "Starting with me."

His eyes narrowed, his expression becoming guarded, wary. "What do ye mean?"

"I told you I'm from America and I told you I came here to study and work in Edinburgh," she said. "All of that is true. What I've not been honest about is *when* I come from."

He studied her face. "Ye aren't making any sense."

Beth took the cell phone from her pocket and turned it on. The battery was running low. It would soon run out and she'd have no way to recharge it. She had to get him to understand before that happened. She scrolled through the apps and found a video she'd downloaded of some puppies. Steeling her courage, she pressed the play button and held it out to Cam.

He eyed it suspiciously. "That's the device ye were looking at in the clearing. Ye didnae want me to see it."

She nodded. "Take it. It's called a cell phone."

Slowly, as if the phone was a viper that might bite him, Cam reached out and took it from her. His eyes widened as he watched the video running on the screen.

"What manner of Fae magic is this? These images are moving! And where does the sound come from?"

"A speaker on the back," Beth replied. "And it's not powered by magic. It's powered by technology."

"I've never seen the like," Cam murmured, his eyes moving as they followed the images flitting across the screen.

"No," Beth replied. She took a deep breath. "Because it hasn't been invented yet. And it won't be invented for another several hundred years."

His eyes snapped up to meet hers. "I dinna understand."

Okay, no going back now. She forced out the words.

"Cam, I'm from the future. When I stepped through Irene MacAskill's archway it sent me back in time. I'm from the twenty-first century."

The words tumbled into a well of silence. She watched Cam intently, awaiting his response. He said nothing. She could almost see his thoughts churning behind his eyes as he put it all together. Her sudden appearance in the forest that day. Her strange clothing. Her odd way of speaking and use of words he didn't understand. Her possession of a device that defied all logic.

"The future?" he whispered at last. "That's yer home?"

"Yes," she nodded. "Which is where I need to get back to."

Cam closed his eyes and breathed deeply for one, two, three breaths. When he opened them again, he seemed to have gathered himself. He handed the phone back to Beth.

"Why did ye not tell me sooner?"

"Would you have believed me?"

He thought about that. "Probably not."

"But you believe me now?"

"How can I not?" he said with a wry smile. "I've just seen light and moving images pour from a tiny box. I canna even begin to imagine how such a thing would work but I know of the magic of the Fae. I dinna doubt they have the power over time and I'm sure Irene is one of them. What I dinna understand is why Irene would send ye back to my time?"

"I don't know," Beth replied. "She said I would find my destiny and help undo a great injustice."

Cam looked at her sharply, an odd expression crossing his face. "She said that?"

"I know, crazy, right?"

"Aye," he whispered, his voice hoarse.

The sun had dipped behind the mountains and now the lake took on the look of steel, gray and unforgiving. The temperature plummeted and Beth wrapped her arms around herself to keep warm. Cam stared out over the lake for a long moment, wrapped in his own thoughts.

"Do ye still want to know the truth about me?" he asked at last. "Last chance, lass. Turn around and return to the house. Ye dinna need to get involved in the mess that is my life."

"I'm already involved," Beth replied. "I told you my truth. Now it's your turn."

He stared at her, his eyes as blue as winter frost, and for a moment she felt herself falling into them. Then he blinked, looked away, and pulled a deep breath through his nostrils.

He held up his arms, showing the faded gray coils of his tattoo. "This isnae at tattoo at all," he said. "It's a brand. The mark of a bargain I once made. A bargain with the Fae."

"The Fae," she breathed. "A few weeks ago I wouldn't have believed in any such thing. Who are they?"

"Fairy creatures older than time itself. They are of the mountains and the rivers. Of the air and the sea. They hold power over the creatures and people of the Highlands and they will exercise that power however they see fit, regardless of the consequences." His eyes fixed on Beth. "As I said, I suspect Irene MacAskill is such a creature."

"You said you met Irene on the same day you met me. Was it then you made this bargain?"

He shook his head. "Nay, it was a long time ago and with another of her kind: a creature that looks like an old man. Several years ago my brother Logan was laird of the MacAuley clan, I was commander of the clan's warriors and my younger brother Finlay was our chief scout and bard. It was a grand time. Our clan prospered. Then rumors reached us of strife in Ireland. Famine. Disease. A rise in banditry and lawlessness. We didnae pay the rumors much heed until Finn came back from a patrol with word of an enormous fleet of raiders making their way across the sea to sack Dun Ringill. Thousands of men bent on destroying my home and taking what they wanted. We were desperate. Even the might of the MacAuley clan couldnae stand against such numbers. My cousin Eoin, who was always a scholar of the old ways, suggested appealing to the Fae. So we did."

His eyes had gone distant, filled with memory. Beth took a step closer, laid her hand on his arm. "What happened?"

He didn't reply for a long time and in his eyes Beth could almost see the churning memories. But finally he began to speak again. "We traveled to a stone circle near Dun Ringill. Such places belong to the Fae. This one was called the stones of Druach. There we called upon the Fae and one answered. The three MacAuley brothers struck a bargain: our lives in return for the power to save our clan. It was granted. The three of us together, filled with power of the Fae, drove off the invaders and then returned to the stone circle to die. But the Fae didnae kill us. He cursed us. Never to know family. Never to know love. Never to be again the men we once were."

He looked down and Beth realized she'd inadvertently placed her hand over his tattoo. It felt slightly warm to the touch.

Cam smiled wryly. "I was once the mightiest warrior of the MacAuley clan and the Fae used my vanity against me. Oh aye, I am a mighty warrior still. But I am cursed with blood-lust, Beth. The rage comes upon me like a fever, like an itch that must be scratched. It demands violence, it demands blood, and I struggle to control it. That's the man ye saw in the inn. The man I've become."

He fell silent. It was full dark and Beth could barely see him now. He was just a silhouette outlined against the backdrop of the lake but she heard his laboured breathing, as though he'd been running for a long time.

"It makes sense now," she murmured. "You being two different men. The one who saved a disabled child and the one who killed that outlaw in the forest."

He shook his head. "I am but one man, lass. The curse only took that dark part of myself and amplified it. It was always there, lurking. Do ye understand why I didnae tell ye? I long to be a good man but know that I am not. Far from it."

"What's the definition of a good man?" she countered. "I once thought I knew. It was easy: there were bad people and good people and the bad ones deserved to be put away. Now? I'm not so sure. Maybe all we can do is strive to do the right thing. "

"What if ye dinna know what the right thing is?"

"Nobody ever said it was easy."

She blew out a sigh and ran a hand through her hair, thinking through all that Cam had told her. A few weeks ago if somebody had claimed that they were cursed, she would have laughed. Any fool knew that curses weren't real. *Yeah,* she thought. *Like time-travel and the Fae aren't real.* She was beginning to learn that not everything was as she'd thought.

"So that's why you were so freaked out when Rabbie said your clan have a new laird," she said, as realization dawned. "Logan MacAuley. Your brother."

"Aye," he replied. "I dinna know how it's possible. He was laird before our bargain and it seems he's found a way to return to it."

"If your brother can break his curse, so can you. We just have to figure out how."

He gave a wry smile that held no conviction. "Nay, lass. I am content. I will guard ye with my life and see ye safe home again—ye have given me a purpose and for that I thank ye."

He took hold of her hands and clasped them to his chest, close to his heart. His hands felt huge and strong around hers, his skin hard and callused, yet warm. He looked down at her, his eyes searching her face.

"I willnae ever harm ye, lass," he breathed. "Ye need not fear me."

"I know that," Beth replied. "I don't know how, but I knew that from the first moment I saw you. Why else would I agree to travel with an uncouth lout?"

A ghost of a smile quirked his lips. "Why indeed?"

Beth found herself staring up at him. His eyes seemed to glow in the gloom like blue lamps, the moonlight that was beginning to seep through the trees casting his face into planes and angles. Beth's pulse quickened. A shiver went down her spine but this time it wasn't from fear or unease.

Cam's lips parted and a low breath escaped him. For one scintillating, terrifying moment Beth thought he would lean down and kiss her, and even more terrifying, for an instant she wanted that more than anything in the world.

But he didn't kiss her. He blinked as if waking from sleep, released her hands and stepped back.

"Come. We should be getting back. Rabbie and Elspeth will think we've gotten lost."

He held out his hand and Beth took it. In silence he led her back through the darkened landscape to the MacGoverns' croft.

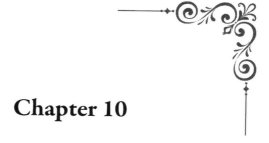

Chapter 10

As they stepped into the glade, Beth saw a campfire burning in a pit several meters in front of the house. Rabbie and Elspeth sat together on a log, Travis perched in his chair next to them. A spit straddled the fire, one of the pheasants Cam had caught that morning slowly roasting over it.

"Ah!" Rabbie called as he spotted them. "There ye are! Perfect timing as ever, my friend. The food is almost cooked."

"Why do ye think I made myself scarce?" Cam replied. "Ye know how much I hate cooking!"

He and Beth seated themselves on a log on the opposite side of the fire. Rabbie passed over two beakers and filled them with whisky.

"Look, Uncle Cam," Travis said, holding something out in both hands. "I've been practicing my letters, just like ye taught me."

He was holding the slate tablet Beth had seen him writing on earlier. It was covered in neat, precise letters.

Cam took the slate and peered at it. "My, little man, ye have a fine hand. Finer than my own, I can tell ye. I've seen nay better work in all the Highlands."

The boy beamed at the compliment. "Does that mean I can be a scribe someday like ye said?"

Cam ruffled the boy's hair. "Any laird would be proud to have ye."

Elspeth leaned close to Beth. "Cam taught him his letters. Neither Rabbie nor I can read. We hope Travis might one day be good enough to earn a place as a scribe. His father and I will-nae be around forever and when we're gone what will happen to him? He canna stay here—not with his difficulties. Cam said he'll do his best to find him a place in a lord's hall when he's old enough."

There was worry in her voice and Beth reached out to squeeze her new friend's shoulder. "Then he will. Cam keeps his word."

Elspeth forced a smile. "Aye, that he does."

"Right!" Rabbie said, rubbing his hands. "I reckon it's ready. Who's for roast pheasant?"

There was a chorus of agreement and Rabbie took the bird from the fire, carved it expertly with his belt knife, before passing it around on wooden plates. There were roasted vegetables to go with it and gravy that Elspeth had made from the pheasant's juices. It was by far the best meal Beth had eaten since she'd come to this time. In fact, as she tucked in, she reflected it was one of the best meals she'd eaten in *any* time. The meat came apart on her tongue and the vegetables were crisp and juicy.

Silence descended as everyone ate, broken only by the crackle of the fire. Rabbie refilled everyone's cup with another dram of whisky. He and Cam had already drunk three or four but neither of them seemed in the least affected by the potent spirit. Which was more than could be said for Beth. Anymore and she'd wake up with a headache. She accepted the cup politely but then set it on the ground by her feet without taking a swig.

Elspeth nodded conspiratorially. "Most wise. Sometimes I reckon Rabbie has whisky for blood and Cam the same. Give me a cup of warm milk any day." She nodded at the ground and Beth looked down to see Elspeth's cup untouched by her feet, just like Beth's.

She snorted a laugh. "I'll introduce you to the delights of cocktails one day. Pina Colada, Mojito, Bellini. Or just a plain old glass of red would do."

After the meal, Rabbie brought out a small stringed instrument a little like a guitar with a rounded body. He nestled the instrument against his chest and plucked at a few of the strings.

"Ah, perfectly in tune," he announced.

He launched into a jaunty melody that had them all tapping their feet and clapping along. After a moment Elspeth started to sing. Her voice was lovely and it melded perfectly with the notes from the instrument. It was some sort of folk song about a brewer and his wife and their efforts to swindle some villagers out of their money. It was bawdy enough in places to make Beth raise her eyebrow and brought plenty of laughs.

When the tune fell silent Rabbie reached behind him and came up holding a wooden flute. "Still reckon ye've got it?" he said to Cam.

"Got it?" Cam said incredulously. "Toss that thing here! I'll show ye who's got it!"

With a grin Rabbie threw the flute over. Much to Beth's astonishment, Cam set the instrument to his lips and began to play. The sound was high and lilting, Cam's fingers moving across the holes expertly. Beth snapped her mouth shut. Would this man ever stop surprising her?

Rabbie listened for a few bars, following the melody, then he joined in with the lute and the two of them played a quick, cheerful tune that Elspeth and Travis clapped along with. After a few bars all three MacGoverns began to sing. Rabbie's voice was rough but Travis's was smooth and sweet, almost as beautiful as his mother's. They sang loudly, grins on their faces, as Rabbie and Cam filled the glade with music. It was an easy tune to follow and the chorus repeated after every verse. Beth listened a few times and then joined in.

It was a long time since Beth had done any singing and her singing voice left a lot to be desired but nobody seemed to mind that. Elspeth shot her a grin and Cam winked at her as she filled her lungs and joined in with this impromptu choir. She soon found herself enjoying it immensely, all cares forgotten in the simple joy of good companionship.

As they all fell about laughing when the song ended, Beth realized she couldn't remember the last time she'd had this much fun. Elspeth, Rabbie and Travis had accepted her without question. They'd welcomed her into their home and treated her like and old friend. She'd known them for only a day and yet she felt utterly at ease.

And then there was Cam. She glanced at him. He was sharing a joke with Travis. The little boy suddenly guffawed with laughter, holding his stomach and doubling over. Something inside her shifted. A feeling stole over her, one she couldn't quite describe. She didn't have anything like this back home. Sure, she had friends but they were all so busy with their jobs and their hectic lives that they never really spent much time together. A quick email, a text and a catch-up at lunchtime were the best they could manage.

But here? Here these people forged bonds that went deeper than friendship. Cam might not be related to the MacGoverns by blood but even so, Beth could see that they were family. They reveled in each other's company, each finding solace and strength from being near the others. It was…wonderful.

Travis let out a huge yawn, stuffing his hand over his mouth to hide it.

Elspeth didn't miss it. "Right! Time for bed, little man!"

"But I'm not tired, Ma!" Travis protested. "Can I stay up a little longer? Beth is gonna tell me all about this hero they have in her land called Spider Man."

"And I will," Beth said with a smile. "In the morning."

Travis nodded reluctantly then bade them all good night and allowed his mother and father to wheel him into the house.

Beth watched them go and then cleared her throat. "Well, I suppose I'd better turn in too. Goodnight, Cam."

He nodded, a small smile curling his lips. "Aye, goodnight, lass."

Beth rose to her feet and crossed to the door. She paused on the threshold and looked back. Cam stared into the flames, his outline a silhouette against the orange. Beth turned away and made her way to the room Elspeth and Rabbie had set aside for her. She suspected that Travis had been turned out of it and now shared with his parents but nobody had said and she was too polite to ask.

She undressed and climbed into the narrow bed. Blowing out the candle, she pulled up the blanket and tried to sleep. Her thoughts turned to Cam. Was he still sitting by the fire? Or had he retired to his own bed in the stable? Was he thinking of her even as she thought of him?

She turned over. *Stop it!* she told herself. *Stop thinking about him! You'll be going home soon and you'd be better off concentrating on that!*

She sat up in bed. It was so dark she could barely see her hand in front of her face and the groan of creaking beams sounded softly as the house settled. Somewhere outside, an owl hooted.

It was no good. Her thoughts were too frenzied for sleep.

Throwing back the blanket, she climbed out of bed and dressed. On cat's paws she crept through the sleeping house and made her way outside. The fire had died down to embers and she saw no sign of Cam. Involuntarily her eyes strayed to the stable. She hesitated. For a moment she was taken with the almost overwhelming urge to go to him.

Instead she crossed the barnyard and took the trail she and Cam had walked that afternoon. Restless energy filled her and she always found that walking helped when her thoughts wouldn't settle. When she'd first come to Scotland after...what happened, she'd often been unable to sleep. She'd found herself wandering the university campus in the small hours with only the foxes for company.

At length she came out onto the banks of the lake. In the moonlight its surface shimmered like quicksilver. With a sigh she flopped onto the bank and propped her chin in her hand, staring out over the darkened landscape as thoughts tumbled through her head like blown leaves.

She didn't know how long she'd sat like that before a noise in the undergrowth startled her from her thoughts. Cam stepped out of the trees.

"My apologies," he said, holding up his hands. "I didnae mean to scare ye." He sat on the bank by her side.

"Couldn't you sleep either?" she asked.

"Nay, I dinna sleep much these days. I got up for some air and saw yer footprints. Damn near broke my ankle tripping over Rabbie's lute on the way," he grumbled.

Remembering their impromptu concert, Beth smiled to herself. "I didn't know you could play the flute."

"Aye," he replied with a smile. "One of my many talents."

"So I see. Who taught you?"

A shadow passed across his face. "My mother. Long ago. She taught all of us. Logan was hopeless. I, only a little better, but Finlay? Ah, ye should hear my little brother play! He has a gift. There isnae an instrument on God's Earth that he could-nae make sing like the angels."

Beth smiled wryly. "When I was little my mother sent me for piano lessons. I hated it. I had this crotchety old instructor who used to whack my fingers with a ruler when I got the notes wrong. Needless to say, I didn't keep it up."

Cam laughed. "Sounds like my old sword-master. Lord, if that man smiled I reckon it would crack his face." He fell silent for a moment but then looked at her quizzically. "What are ye doing out here, lass?"

"I don't know," she replied. "Thinking."

"About what?"

About how confused I am, Beth thought. *About how I ought to be desperate to go home but I'm not. How that thought terrifies me*.

But she didn't say any of this. She just shrugged then went back to staring at the water.

"Ye know," Cam said after a moment. "That is the first time ye've told me anything about yer kin, lass. They must be missing ye dearly by now."

Beth said nothing. His words stirred unwelcome feelings. She thought back to the easy camaraderie the MacGoverns had shown around the camp fire. It had reminded her how much she was missing. How empty her life had become.

But returning home won't fix that, she thought. *Not anymore*.

Cam waited patiently without speaking.

She gathered a deep breath. Oh god. She didn't want to talk about this. She *never* wanted to talk about this. But something about Cam's calm, reassuring presence made the words come bubbling to the surface.

"I have no family. I was an only child and my parents died when I was eighteen."

Cam sucked in a breath. "Ah, lass. I'm sorry. What happened?"

The memory opened in her mind like a diseased bud and she was powerless to stop it. She remembered the bite of the cold wind as she'd opened the door that winter night. She remembered the expressions on the faces of the police officers standing there. She remembered the sick dread that had filled her stomach because she knew...she knew what they were going to say...

"They were killed," she told Cam. "Murdered as they walked home after going to the theater. And for what?" She couldn't keep the anger and bitterness from seeping into her voice. "For a few hundred dollars that my dad had in his wallet. That's why I came to Scotland—to escape the memories. That's why I trained to be a lawyer, so that I could spend my life putting people like those who took my parents behind bars and standing up to injustice wherever I found it."

Camdan said nothing for a moment. Then he let out a long, low breath. "Ah, lass. I'm sorry. Sorry that happened to ye. Sorry ye have to put up with a man like me. I must embody everything ye loathe."

She looked at him sharply. Loathe? Hardly. Yes, when she'd first met him she'd thought him the worst kind of thug, the kind of man she would happily see rotting in a jail cell. But now? Now she'd gotten to know him?

"You scared me to start with," she admitted. "Imagine it: the first person I meet in this time is some crazy, plaid-wearing, sword-swinging maniac who's doing his best to chop bits off people."

"And yet ye came to my aid anyway," Cam observed with a smile. "That was either brave or stupid."

"Oh, definitely stupid," Beth replied. "I've never claimed to be brave."

He raised an eyebrow. "I beg to differ. Ye are one of the bravest people I've ever met."

Right now Beth didn't feel brave. She felt terrified and it had nothing to do with Fae or curses or traveling through time. She was terrified because the way Cam was looking at her sent a tingle right down her spine and caused her heart to flutter in her chest.

He reached out and brushed a strand of hair away from her face. "And now?" he asked gently. "Do I still scare ye?"

"Only with your singing," she replied.

Cam bellowed a laugh, the sound of it rumbling out into the night and lifting Beth's heart. "Aye, I think I probably deserved that. Didnae I tell ye that it's Finlay who's the singer?"

She smiled. "Well, we all have our cross to bear." Then she sobered abruptly. "But in answer to your question: no, you don't scare me anymore. You make me feel safe, Cam."

And alive, she wanted to add. *And full of joy and wonder. You make me feel things I never knew existed.*

"I'm mighty glad to hear ye say that," he breathed. He brushed the tips of his fingers across her cheek. Only the lightest of touches, little more than a whisper, but the contact sent a tremor through her body.

"Cam, I—"

She didn't get any further. Camdan leaned close and kissed her.

For a moment she went rigid with shock. For a moment. Then her body responded. As his mouth covered hers she scooted closer, allowed Cam to catch her in his arms and press her tight against him. His lips were warm, his kiss hard and insistent. It lit her body like a torch.

Her nerves roared into raging, glorious life. She was suddenly minutely aware of every place his body touched hers: his strong arms around her waist, the palms of his hands pressing into her back, his lips soft and insistent against hers.

Before she knew it, her tongue was dancing with his and her fingers had tangled in his red-gold hair. Lord help her, but she'd never wanted any man like she wanted Cam right now.

But Cam pulled back suddenly. In the moonlight she saw that his eyes had gone dark, his pupils huge. Raw desire shone in them, barely contained.

"Beth," he said, his voice low and husky with need. "I will-nae be able to stop myself if this goes any further. If ye wish to stop, ye must say so now." His voice trembled, on the edge of control.

"I don't want you to stop," she gasped.

It was all the invitation he needed. With a growl he yanked her against him, his kiss fierce and full of passion. Beth answered him with equal ardor, knotting her fists in the front of his plaid and pulling him close. Her fingers found their way to the knot that tied his plaid and she tugged frantically at the bindings until they came loose and the plaid fell away, exposing his naked chest in the moonlight.

The contours of his chest were filled with light and shadow, the myriad little scars showing white against the darkness. To Beth they were beautiful. Gently she ran her fingertips across his chest, tracing the line of the scars, and Cam shuddered under her touch.

He pushed her down into the grass, pinning her beneath him as his lips caressed her neck and his hands trailed lower, tracing the line of her belly and hips. His touch was electric. She wanted to feel his skin against hers, wanted nothing between them but their own body heat.

Cam had the same idea. He gripped the laces that held closed the bodice of Beth's dress and tugged savagely. She heard a ripping sound as the fabric tore slightly then the garment came loose and Cam pushed it impatiently off her shoulders. Beth shivered as her breasts were exposed to the cool night air, sending goose bumps riding across her pale skin. But the discomfort was replaced by searing heat a moment later as Cam bent and took one nipple in his mouth.

Beth gasped, arching under him as his tongue licked and flicked, his other hand tracing a line of fire down her hip. Taking the bunched up dress in both hands, Cam tugged it down and Beth obliged by wriggling out of it completely. She felt not in the least embarrassed as Cam looked her over with an expression of raw, naked lust. In fact, she felt emboldened, more free than she ever had before.

There was no doubting how much Cam wanted her. Desire rolled off him in waves and the way his plaid tented around his groin was testament to his urgent desire.

But he held himself back. He bent slowly to lay gentle caresses on her stomach, kisses that made her shudder as tingles of electricity writhed right through her body. Pleased with her reaction, Cam's kisses traveled lower, down to her navel and back up again. It was too much. Beth grabbed his shoulders, pulled him down atop her.

Cam obeyed her silent command. Nudging her knees apart, he positioned himself between her legs, propping himself up with hands to either side of her head so he could look down at her. Then, with a thrust of his hips, he drove himself inside her. Beth cried out as their bodies joined, Cam filling her completely. They began to move against each other. Cam's muscles bunched and relaxed as he drove inside, slowly at first but with an increasing tempo, and Beth matched his movements, her fingers digging into the hard muscles of his shoulders as her hips ground against his.

His eyes, normally so pale, had gone so dark as to seem almost black, glittering with reflected moonlight but his tattoo, Beth noticed, was beginning to glow. Its heat matched his passion and as its power increased so too did the urgency of Cam's lovemaking. He took Beth with him. Never in her life had she experienced the all-consuming sensations that his body provoked in hers. Every nerve seemed to come alive, her veins filling with liquid fire.

He thrust into her and she arched under him, her nails digging into his skin as she finally, irrevocably reached her climax. Screaming his name to the stars, Beth shuddered beneath him and came apart, all sense of self obliterated by the tide of bliss he swept her up in.

A moment later he shuddered and reached his own climax, letting out a gasp that was more like the low, guttural snarl of a wolf. For the longest moment he held himself inside her and she clung to him, eyes screwed tight shut as she tried to piece together her fragmented thoughts and regain control.

Finally, after a passage of time she couldn't measure, the euphoria began to ebb and Beth came back to herself. She opened her eyes to find Cam gazing down at her. His tattoo was no longer glowing and the raw lust was gone from his eyes, to be replaced by a warmth that made Beth's stomach flip. Holy shit, but he was beautiful.

She reached up and cupped his face with one hand. He said not a word, only turned his head and kissed her hand before slowly leaning down and pressing his lips to her forehead. Then he rolled away to grab his plaid before laying it over them both.

He wrapped his arms around her, pulling her against him in a protective embrace. Beth rested her head on his shoulder and Cam kissed the top of her head.

"Beth," he murmured into her hair. "Are ye all right? I didnae hurt ye?"

"No," she murmured, tipping her head back and softly kissing the line of stubble along his jaw. "You didn't hurt me."

He smiled at her. "Ye are beautiful. So beautiful. Ye set my blood afire, lass. What witchery have ye cast on me?"

Beth didn't answer. Instead she continued laying kisses along his jawline and then down his neck to his hard chest. Cam groaned, his breath escaping him in a hiss.

"You mean *that* kind of witchery?" Beth said, arching an eyebrow.

"Aye," he breathed, rolling towards her. "That's exactly what I mean. Now come here, my little witch."

Beth giggled as he grabbed her then his kiss robbed her of the ability to speak. Arousal flared and everything else was forgotten.

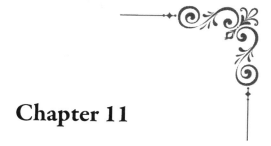

Chapter 11

Cam woke just as dawn light was starting to filter through the trees. He opened his eyes to a clear sky and streamers of mist rising off the lake. He shifted his weight and Beth, snuggled close against his side, groaned softly but didn't wake.

Cam gazed down at her, still hardly able to believe that last night had really happened, that it hadn't been some dream his mind had conjured up to torture him with what he most fervently desired. But here she was: whole and real and naked next to him, her weight against his chest a luxury that made his stomach tighten with joy.

Beth was his. His! A stupid grin spread across his face but he didn't try to stop it. Reaching down, careful not to wake her, he gently swept a loose strand of chestnut hair from across her face. Her eyes were closed, her breathing even. Heaven above, but she was beautiful. The first light of the day caught her face, accentuating her cheekbones and the freckles that covered her nose. Her lips were plump and full and ripe for kissing.

Cam resisted the urge. Even now, as he watched her sleep, he felt his ardor rise. How many times had he claimed her last night? How many times had they made love in the soft grass? He had no idea. His memories were a jumble of searing heat, desperate passion, and a sense of completeness that Cam had never dreamed possible.

What is this? he thought to himself. *I've never felt anything like it. What's happening to me? To us?*

The deep, desperate ache to be near her, the euphoria that filled him when she smiled, the heady sense of being able to achieve anything when she was with him was a feeling totally alien to Cam. He wasn't inexperienced. In his life Cam had known many women. But none of them had stirred in Cam the feelings that were coursing through his blood right now. None of those women had ever made him feel so...alive.

It canna be, a voice whispered in the back of his head. *She is from the future and she will return there when she gets the chance. Dinna get close to a woman ye are going to lose.*

The thought of a future without her sent a spear of panic right through him, but he pushed the thought away, refused to listen to the voice. Today was today. Let tomorrow worry about itself.

Unable to resist any longer, he bent his head and kissed her softly on the lips. Her eyes fluttered open and her face broke into a smile.

"Well, that's a 'good morning' I could get used to."

He shrugged. "Well, I had to find some way to stop ye from snoring."

She pushed herself onto her elbows, her hair spilling down her chest. "I was *not* snoring!"

"Nay? My mistake. It must have been a wild boar rooting around in the undergrowth."

"Lout!" she swung at him playfully and he caught her wrist.

Then suddenly he was kissing her again and she was responding, the plaid falling down until there was nothing between their bodies but heat. Oh, Lord help him, he couldn't get enough of this woman.

It took every ounce of his battle-trained self-control to break the kiss. "We'd better be heading back," he said gruffly. "We've a long road ahead of us today."

She nodded reluctantly and they rose from their makeshift bed and quickly dressed. Taking Beth's hand, he led her back through the trees to Elspeth and Rabbie's croft.

As he'd expected, they found their friends up and working, even though the sun had yet to fully rise over the horizon. Elspeth stood on the veranda, beating a rug that was hanging from a line whilst Rabbie was chopping wood. Young Travis had a ball of twine balanced in his lap and appeared to be weaving a net for his da.

They looked up as Cam and Beth stepped out of the trees. A grin flashed across Rabbie's face, quickly stifled, and Elspeth shared a fleeting, knowing look with her husband. Seeing this exchange, Beth blushed scarlet, but Cam had to stop himself from grinning. He didn't care who knew what had happened between himself and Beth last night. Lord, he wanted to shout it at the top of his voice!

"Uncle Cam!" Travis exclaimed. "Ye weren't in the barn when I went to look for ye. Have ye and Beth been for a walk?"

Beth's blush deepened, if that was possible, and Cam quickly came to her rescue. He bounded over to where Travis was sitting and ruffled the lad's hair.

"Aye, lad. And what have ye got there? My, that is a mighty fine net. I'm sure yer Da will catch all sorts of game in it."

"He might if Uncle Cam helps him finish chopping this firewood," Rabbie called. "My back is fair aching!"

Whilst Elspeth and Beth made their way into the house Cam walked over to where Rabbie leaned on his ax by the wood pile. His friend raised an eyebrow.

"Ye look different but I canna quite put my finger on it. Ah, I've got it! Ye are smiling! Lord above, it's a terrifying sight!"

Cam snorted a laugh, picked up the ax and began splitting logs. "Aye, well. I find I have much to smile about this morning."

"I would imagine ye do if yer empty bed is aught to go by." Rabbie regarded his friend with an earnest expression. "I'm nay surprised. It was obvious from the first moment ye arrived how ye felt about the lass."

Cam stopped and leaned on the ax. "It was?"

"Aye, to anyone that knows ye," Rabbie replied. "I'm happy for ye, my friend. She's a fine woman."

"Aye," Cam agreed. "She is that."

Rabbie cocked his head. "What about when ye reach Edinburgh? Surely ye willnae let her leave?"

A stab of something hard and cold went right through Cam. The future he'd avoided thinking about suddenly loomed in his mind. Let her go? How could he? But equally, how could he ask her to stay? What did he have to offer a woman like her? It suddenly felt as though a fist had wrapped itself around his heart and was squeezing tight.

"I must let her leave for her own sake. What else can I do?" he said. "I'm a mercenary. A hired killer. That isnae any kind of life for her."

"Ye *were* a mercenary," Rabbie corrected. "That doesnae mean ye have to remain one forever. There are always other paths to take, other roads to tread."

Cam's eyes narrowed at his friend's words. They sounded eerily like those Irene MacAskill had spoken to him that night on the trail. Could Rabbie be right? Could there be another path for him? A future that included Beth?

Rabbie patted him on the shoulder. "Think on it, my friend. Sometimes ye must take risks if ye want to be happy. Look at me —I thought Elspeth's da would just about kill me when I asked for her hand but I was willing to risk his wrath for her. Mayhap ye must do the same."

Cam took a deep breath, glancing at the door through which Beth had gone. His heart thudded with a mixture of hope and fear. Dare he ask her to stay? Dare he take the risk?

WHEN SHE AND CAM HAD approached the holding only to find Elspeth and Rabbie waiting, both clearly cognizant of what she and Cam had been doing, Beth thought she would just about die of embarrassment.

As she followed Elspeth inside, she was grateful that her new friend didn't ask questions. Instead, she folded Beth into a warm embrace.

"Ah, I'm going to miss ye," she said. "It's been wonderful getting to know ye. I wish ye could have stayed longer."

Beth returned the embrace, finding herself suddenly reluctant to leave. She would miss her new friend dearly.

"Me too," she muttered. "Thanks for everything, Elspeth."

"Ye are most welcome, my dear." She gave Beth a sly smile. "And I canna tell ye how pleased I am for ye and Cam. Ye make a fine pair and I dinna reckon I've ever seen such a sparkle in our Cam's eye."

Beth nodded, embarrassed all over again. Together she and Elspeth packed the saddlebags, and Travis came inside to help. The little boy seemed morose that she and Cam were leaving and had a sullen face as he folded clothing and slipped it inside the saddlebags.

Beth knelt down in front of him. "Now then, little man," she said, "we'll have none of that sad face. I want to go on my way remembering that beaming smile of yours."

He nodded although he didn't smile. "Will ye come back and see us soon?"

Beth cast an anxious look at Elspeth who smoothly stepped in. "Come now, my boy, ye know Beth has a long journey to her homeland but I hope she'll remember us often."

"Of course I will," Beth said around a sudden lump in her throat. "As I hope you'll remember me?"

Travis gave a sniffle and said that he would and Beth wrapped her arms around him, holding the little boy close.

Then suddenly it was time to leave the croft behind. Beth hugged them all one last time and then mounted Firefly in front of Cam who nudged the horse into a walk. As they reached the edge of the clearing Beth swiveled in her seat, gazed back at the three figures receding into the distance, and waved.

Then they passed into the trees and the lonely croft was lost from sight. Beth let out a sigh.

"What is it, lass?" Cam asked.

"I only knew them for a short time," Beth replied. "But I'll miss them."

They rode for several hours. This time, Beth leaned back against Cam, reveling in the sensation of his chest against her back. For his part, Cam gripped the reins in one hand, his other arm around Beth's waist protectively. Every so often he would lean forward and plant a light kiss on her neck, sending tingles along her spine.

It was a beautiful morning. The sky above the mountains was a pale blue, just like Cam's eyes, and the air was still and clear. She and Cam could have been the only people in the whole world.

Even so, Cam didn't relax his vigilance. His sword was strapped across his back, a bow attached to the saddle, and his eyes were moving continually, scanning the trail ahead for any hint of danger. Sometimes he would pull Firefly to a halt abruptly and stand in his stirrups, head cocked as if listening. But they encountered nothing and nobody and Beth began to hope that maybe Rabbie's warnings were unfounded.

They made their way gradually higher into the mountain passes and the deciduous trees of the lower slopes were replaced by evergreens that towered high into the sky and left a thick coating of needles on the ground that deadened the sound of the horse's hooves. Cam called a halt well before sundown and they made camp by a meandering river that wound its lazy way between the trees.

They dismounted and fell into the routine of making camp. Whilst Cam saw to Firefly Beth erected the tent, laid out the bedrolls—both inside the tent this time—and started a fire.

Cam crouched and began rooting around in the saddle-bags, inspecting their provisions. After a moment he glanced from the saddlebag to the river and back again.

"Ye know, it would be a shame to waste this opportunity. I know Elspeth has packed us plenty of food but that needs to last all the way to Edinburgh. I think I will avail myself of the chance to catch something fresh."

Beth raised an eyebrow. "I didn't know you were a trapper."

Cam took several poles from the saddlebag that were about as long as his forearm. He slotted them together to form one longer rod and held it up triumphantly. "I'm not. But I *am* a fisherman."

He climbed to his feet and made his way over to the river bank. Beth watched him, smiling at his boyish enthusiasm. Jeez, there were so many sides to that man: the brooding, dangerous warrior, the expert woodsman, the relaxed talented musician, the carefree fisherman. Beth wanted to explore them all, all the many layers that made up this frightening, dangerous, extraordinary man.

She started a fire and finished making camp then stood with her hands on hips, surveying her handiwork. It would do. Satisfied, she made her way over to the riverbank where Cam was perched on a rock, the line arching out over the water. Here the river was wide and sluggish and shallow enough that Beth could see the pebbly bottom. Fish—salmon at a guess—could be seen meandering along but as yet not one of them seemed interested in Cam's bait.

She sat on the rock next to him. "My dad took me fishing once. I could never get the hang of it and they kept wriggling off the line."

"It's easy," he told her. "Let me show ye."

He handed her the rod. It was constructed of willow withies, making it extremely flexible. A line made from some sort of sinew was attached to the pole.

"Hold it here," Cam instructed, taking her hands and moving them into the desired position. He seated himself behind her then scooted forward so that she nestled between his outstretched legs. Like this he could reach around and guide her hands.

His fingers rested on hers, warm and rough. He was incredibly close, his breath hot and heavy on the back of her neck and the nearness of him sent her thoughts scattering like leaves blown in the breeze.

"Sorry, what did you say?"

"Hold it like this," Cam repeated. "Not too much pressure. There will be a tug when ye have a bite and then ye will have to be quick to reel him in."

He spoke like an instructor to a student but he didn't remove his hands from hers or make any effort to move away. Nor did Beth want him to. She found herself leaning back against him, breathing in the scent of him: that unique mix of leather, sweat and pine needles that was so quintessentially him. His thumb moved, gently stroking the length of her finger.

"Are you deliberately trying to put me off?" she demanded. "We won't catch anything at this rate."

"My apologies," he said and she could hear the smile in his voice.

Just then she felt a tug on the line. With a cry of excitement she surged to her feet. "I've got something!"

The tug grew stronger and Beth found herself overbalancing. She tried to right herself but her foot slipped. Dropping the line, her arms pin-wheeling, she tried to regain her balance, but there was nothing to grab onto and with a yelp she went crashing into the river.

It was cold! Icy fingers clawed at her skin and she gasped in shock. She came up spluttering and puffing, getting her feet under her. The water only reached her waist. She shook her head to clear her eyes only to see Cam holding his stomach as he doubled over in laughter.

Outraged indignation welled up inside her. Damn the man! What was so funny about getting a dunking in a freezing mountain river? She resisted the urge to swear at him. Instead she crossed her arms and raised an eyebrow.

"Finished?"

He straightened, getting a hold of his mirth with some effort. "I'm sorry, lass," he said in a voice that didn't sound sorry at all. "But that was priceless."

She scowled at him. "Are you just going to stand there or are you going to help me out?" She held out a hand.

Cam edged down the slippery bank and curled his hand around her wrist. Marshalling her strength, Beth gave an almighty heave. Cam let out a strangled yelp and then crashed into the water right by her side, coming up coughing and spluttering and with a look on his face every bit as outraged as hers.

"Now *that* was priceless," Beth said.

Cam's outraged expression transformed into a wide, mischievous grin. Catching her around the waist, he pulled her against him and kissed her. Beth melted into him, her arms going around his neck, the cold water swirling around her hips suddenly forgotten as heat flooded through her body. She ran her fingers through his wet hair and his arms tightened around her, crushing her against his chest.

He bent and lifted her into his arms easily, as if she weighed no more than a doll. He carried her from the water and back to their campsite, all thoughts of fishing forgotten. Cam laid Beth by the fire and suddenly they were pulling at each other's clothes, stripping off the wet garments and tossing them away.

Beth barely noticed the cold air that brushed her skin—all she needed to keep warm was Cam's body against hers. She pulled him down atop her, kissing him fiercely, her fingers sweeping down his back to his buttocks and then up again. Then all thoughts were forgotten as they made love slowly while the firelight dried their skin.

Chapter 12

The next morning Beth woke up alone. The space Cam had occupied in the tent was empty, all trace of his warmth gone. She went still, listening, and from outside came the sound of him moving around the camp and softly humming.

She smiled to herself then stretched, trying to ease the heavy, satisfied lassitude that filled her limbs. Throwing back the blanket, she crawled to the tent door and looked out. Cam was brushing down Firefly. He had his back to her but Beth didn't doubt he knew she was watching him—he missed nothing—but he didn't pause in his work. Firefly stood placidly as Cam brushed out his tail and then examined each of his hooves before leading him in a slow circle, inspecting his gait with a critical eye.

"Everything okay?" Beth asked, exiting the tent.

Cam glanced at her and smiled. "Aye. Well enough. He needs new shoes but they'll last long enough for us to reach Edinburgh. We'll cross the mountains today. Tomorrow we'll come down on the Edinburgh road."

Beth's smile faltered. Tomorrow? So soon? A cold shiver slid down her back and it had nothing to do with the cool morning air. Today was her last day alone with Cam. Oh god, how was she supposed to deal with that?

He frowned. "Are ye well, lass? Ye look pale."

"I'm fine," she said, forcing a smile.

He paused for a moment and looked as though he wanted to say something. Beth waited. *Ask me to stay,* she thought. *Ask me to stay and I will. I don't want to leave you. Not now. Not ever.*

For one, two, three heartbeats he stared at her, a deep longing in his eyes. Then he turned back to the horse.

Beth sighed. Her last day alone with Cam. Tomorrow they would be on the Edinburgh road. What had been a beautiful morning now seemed gray and desolate. How could anything in the twenty-first century compare to the last few days?

With a heavy heart she went through her morning ablutions, packed up the camp, and then sat down with Cam and had fried sausage for breakfast. She ate mechanically, hardly tasting the food, her mind elsewhere.

Misreading her mood Cam said, "Dinna worry, lass. We'll make it through the mountains all right and ye'll reach Edinburgh safe and well."

She forced a smile. "I know."

They mounted up and left. As always Beth sat in front of Cam but she took the reins this time and guided Firefly along the trail as Cam directed. Through their days of journeying she'd become much more comfortable with the formidable warhorse and for his part the stallion seemed to have decided he could trust her. He no longer flattened his ears or bared his teeth when she came near. Cam, freed of the burden of guiding the horse, rode with his hands resting lightly on Beth's hips. It was very distracting.

They were approaching a narrow cut through two peaks. High cliffs on either side made the cut more like a ravine and it was towards this pass that the trail climbed in a zig-zag pattern. Finally, the trees pulled back and were replaced by scraggly bushes not much taller than Firefly's knees. There was little cover now and the temperature was markedly colder, the breeze tugging at Beth's hair and sending icy drafts down her neck.

Cam grew tenser as they rode. His tattoo was a stark, brilliant black, more noticeable than it had been for the last few days. Beth could sense the rage of his curse building in him again, from the harsh set of his shoulders to the intense look in his eyes as he scanned the terrain.

"What is it?" she asked. She looked around, trying to figure out what had him on edge but all she could see was the empty vista of the scrubby landscape and the towering peaks of the mountains.

"Nothing," he replied, his voice low and gruff. "But I feel...something."

Cam took back Firefly's reins and they rode in silence. The layer of soil covering the ground became thinner and thinner until it peeled back entirely and they rode over bare slate. The clopping of Firefly's hooves on the hard stone sounded as loud as gunshots in the still mountain air.

They reached the cut, little more than a narrow defile through rock probably left here by the passing of some ancient river millennia ago. The walls on either side were higher than their heads so the whole thing formed a dank, dark tunnel.

Cam pulled Firefly to a halt, his icy blue eyes narrowed as he took in their path. Slowly, he reached over his shoulder and drew his sword, the slither of steel loud in the stillness.

"Something doesnae feel right," he whispered. "We'll go another route." He pulled on the reins, guiding Firefly back a few steps but at that moment a voice suddenly rang out above them.

"I knew ye would come back to me, Cam!"

Men suddenly materialized from gaps in the rock that Beth would have sworn weren't big enough to hide them, a band of ten, twenty, armed men. They spilled across the trail in front and behind, blocking escape. A moment later a man stepped out onto a ledge above the defile. He was tall with black hair tied at his neck and wore a brace of knives strapped around his waist.

"Welcome home, Cam!" the man shouted, opening his arms wide.

Cam's lip pulled back in a snarl. "MacGregor," he growled. "What, by all that's holy, are ye doing up here?"

The man jumped lightly down from the ledge. He wore leather gloves that reached all the way up to his elbows and walked with a slight limp. Even so, he was an imposing figure. Taller even than Cam, he was broad-shouldered and had a thick, bull neck. He looked them over appraisingly and Beth suspected a shrewd intelligence behind that calculating gaze.

"Is that any way to greet an old friend?" the man asked.

"Ye are no friend of mine, MacGregor," Cam replied.

MacGregor walked towards them and Cam's sword hissed out, coming to rest mere inches from the man's throat. "Take another step and I'll skewer ye."

MacGregor's men drew weapons, the whoosh of steel sounding loud in the cold air.

MacGregor smiled. "There isnae need for that, lads. Put up yer swords. Our Camdan has returned to us. I think I can forgive a little fit of temper."

The men followed his orders and sheathed their blades but didn't step back. Glancing around, Beth found twenty pairs of hostile eyes glaring at her. The men were rough and unkempt, obviously outlaws. She swallowed against the sudden fear that tightened her throat.

"Stand aside, MacGregor," Cam said. "And let us be on our way."

"Us?" His eyes flicked to Beth and a leer split his face. "My, my, Cam, ye've got yerself a mighty pretty one this time." He gave Beth a flourishing bow. "Robert MacGregor at yer service, my lady." He spread his arms wide. "Welcome to my kingdom."

"What are ye doing here?" Cam demanded. "Last I heard ye were plying yer trade far to the west and making a tidy profit by all accounts."

MacGregor's eyes snapped back to Cam and his easy smile vanished. "Aye, *was* making a tidy profit. Until the damned MacAuley laird took it into his head to clean up his borders. He and his vaunted MacAuley warriors attacked my stronghold, arrested those they captured, killed those who fought back, and drove the rest of us out." His voice was bitter and angry. "If I ever get my hands on Logan MacAuley, I will make him watch while I kill all of his loved ones!"

Cam said nothing but at mention of his brother his grip on his sword tightened so much that his knuckles turned white. Beth guessed that this band of ruffians didn't know of Cam's relationship with Laird MacAuley and it was best that it stayed that way.

"Stand aside," Cam said again.

MacGregor smiled faintly. "Fight for me. There hasnae been anyone near as good as ye. I will make ye a rich man."

"Are ye deaf?" Cam growled through gritted teeth. "Let us pass."

MacGregor stared hard at Cam, a muscle twitching in his jaw. Cam held his gaze, barely breathing, every muscle in his body coiled like a spring. The threat of violence hung in the air between them. Beth's pulse hammered in her throat. Making a run for it was impossible—the outlaws had blocked every avenue of escape. She bit her lip. Oh hell, how were they going to get out of this?

Then suddenly MacGregor grinned. "Very well. As ye wish. Ye canna blame a man for trying. Pay the toll for passage through my kingdom and ye can be on yer way."

Without taking his eyes off MacGregor Cam reached into the saddlebag and pulled out a bag of coins. "Take it. Then get out of my way."

MacGregor shook his head. "I'm nay interested in yer coin. I'll take another form of payment." He pointed at Beth. "I'll take her."

A twang sounded and an arrow suddenly embedded itself in the meat of Cam's leg. With a grunt, he slumped forward.

"Cam!" Beth screamed.

She tried to turn in the saddle to help him but two of the outlaws darted forward and grabbed Firefly's reins. The warhorse lashed out, rearing and flailing his hooves. The unexpected movement sent Beth slamming back into Cam, her weight sending them both toppling off the back of the horse to smack into the hard ground with enough impact to knock the breath from her lungs.

Sucking in a ragged breath, Beth scrambled onto her knees and crawled over to Cam. The black-feathered arrow shaft was sticking out of his thigh with blood pooling around the wound. With a grimace of pain, he was trying to stand.

"Are you all right?" he asked her.

She nodded, unable to speak as she grabbed his arm and helped him to his feet.

"Get behind me," he instructed.

But two men suddenly grabbed her. Kicking and screaming, they pulled her away from Cam.

"Let her go!" Cam bellowed.

He launched himself after her but the rest of the outlaws converged on him, aiming kicks and punches in his direction. Despite his injured leg, Cam dodged them all. He was faster, more agile than any of them, and each of their blows was answered with a riposte of his own. He ducked under a swinging blow to land a fist into a man's chin. He caught the foot of a man trying to kick him and twisted savagely. The man howled as his knee popped and he crashed to the ground.

Cam's tattoo was glowing white-hot and Beth realized that the rage was on him again. His lips were pulled back in a snarl and there was an animal-like savagery in his eyes as he fought, unarmed, against a seemingly never ending tide of attackers.

The two men held her arms in a tight grip and no matter how hard she struggled she couldn't break it.

"Let me go, damn you!" she yelled.

MacGregor came sidling over. His thumbs were hooked in his belt and he was watching Cam fight his men with a look of satisfaction on his face.

"Quite something isnae he?" he said to Beth. "I've never seen the like." Then he drew one of the daggers strapped around his waist and pressed the point against Beth's throat. She froze, the razor-sharp metal feeling like ice against her skin.

"Stop!" MacGregor shouted to Cam. "Or I will slit yer woman's throat."

Cam froze when he saw the blade and dropped his arms to his sides. The wild look in his eyes retreated and was replaced by something else: fear.

"Let her go," he said in a breathy whisper. "This is between ye and I. It has naught to do with her."

"I think not," MacGregor said. "I think mayhap she will come with us. Call her collateral. Or the spoils of victory."

He nodded to one of his men who swung the flat of his blade against the backs of Cam's legs. With a cry, he collapsed onto his knees, flesh blood running from the arrow wound. The man stepped forward and clubbed Cam across the head with the hilt of his sword. Cam collapsed bonelessly to the ground.

"Cam!" Beth whispered. "Oh my god, Cam!"

"Tie her up," MacGregor ordered. "And somebody bring the horse."

"What about him?" said the one who'd hit Cam.

"Leave him here," MacGregor replied. "When he comes around maybe he'll have thought better of crossing me."

With that the outlaws bound Beth's hands tightly in front of her and dragged her through the defile. She looked over her shoulder, hoping desperately that Cam would suddenly climb to his feet and come after her. But he didn't and his still form was soon lost in the gloom behind them.

"TRY THAT AGAIN AND I'll gag ye," the man growled.

Beth glared at him. It was her third attempt to bite him as he tightened the ropes around her wrists.

"Go to hell!"

The man, a great fat bear of a man with a greasy black beard, scowled at her. "Ye need to learn some manners, woman. Mayhap I'll be the one to teach ye!" He raised his fist but Mac-Gregor barked an order.

"Dinna touch her!" The outlaw leader stalked over, grabbed Beth's bindings and yanked her towards him. "Anyone who harms the wench will answer to me. She remains untouched and unmolested. Clear?"

He glowered around at his men, staring them into submission. Beth took the opportunity to take a breather and look at her surroundings. She remembered little of the journey. She'd fought and kicked all the way until eventually they'd blindfolded her and one of them had carried her slung over his shoulder like a sack of onions. It was only in the last few moments that she'd heard someone mention that they were home then they'd set her on her feet and removed the blindfold.

Beth blinked in surprise. A castle stood in front of them, its battlements and crenulations looking like grinning teeth against the gray sky. But on closer inspection Beth amended that the building *used* to be a castle. It looked ancient and many of its walls and turrets were little more than broken ruins. Fresh thatch covering some of the lower buildings attested to hastily made repairs. Torches burned to either side of the gate and light glowed in some of the windows.

Beth gulped. She couldn't have dreamt up a more forbidding place if she tried.

"Let me go," she said to MacGregor. "I have to go back and help Cam."

MacGregor gave a low, throaty laugh. "I can see why he likes ye. Ye have some spirit, woman, I'll give ye that. What's yer name?"

Beth merely glared at him. MacGregor yanked savagely on the ropes until they dug into her wrists, making her gasp in pain.

"It will go easier for ye if ye do as I say. Ye are hardly in a position to be defiant, are ye? There are over fifty men in that fortress, all of whom would take their sport with ye before slitting yer throat. I am the only thing that stands in their way. I suggest ye do as I say."

Beth's stomach tightened in fear. "Beth. My name is Beth."

"See, that wasnae so hard was it? Well, Beth, ye are going to be visiting with us for a while so I suggest ye stop yammering and behave yerself. "

They began moving again, hurrying down a rocky trail, under the archway of the main gate, and into the fortress proper. Beth guessed that the castle had once guarded the high pass that led through the mountains. From here she could see the landscape spreading out for miles and miles, all the way to the lowlands where lochs glimmered and chimney smoke marked out settlements. It looked a very long way away.

Perhaps in earlier times the castle had rung to the sound of life and laughter but now it was as gloomy and forbidding as a graveyard. As they passed into the repaired interior Beth saw grimy floors covered by reed mats, damp walls that smelled of mildew and fires burning in braziers that gave off oily smoke.

MacGregor had not been exaggerating when he said he had fifty men in this fortress. There was that number at least, all hard-looking outlaws in ragged plaid who squatted around guttering fires or played dice in the drafty, echoing rooms.

MacGregor led Beth through a ruined doorway and she found herself stepping into a large courtyard. She came to a halt, staring. A large wooden cage filled the courtyard around which were rows of wooden benches, all empty.

"What's that?" Beth asked.

"Ye'll see," MacGregor replied. "This way."

He yanked on her bonds, forcing her to follow him.

"How do you know Cam?" she asked.

He glanced at her. "We're old friends."

"Friends?" she asked incredulously. "If that's how you treat your friends I'd hate to be an enemy."

He spun suddenly and she almost walked right into him. He grabbed her under the chin, forced her to look up at him. This close his breath stank of sour wine.

"I'll wager ye think ye know Camdan MacAuley," he said, his voice barely above a whisper. "I'll wager ye think ye are special to him. Let me tell ye a truth, woman: ye aren't. He has fooled ye, as he fools so many. If ye truly knew him ye wouldnae be riding through the mountains alone with such a man."

Beth yanked her chin from his grip and stepped back a pace. "What do you know about it? Nothing!"

He raised an eyebrow. "Ye reckon? Let me ask ye this: did he tell ye that he and I used to be partners? That together we terrorized the northern Highlands? That he was the most feared brigand of them all? Travelers would pay priests to pray for them the night before they set out, hoping that God would spare them the wrath of the Demon Blade. Did he tell ye that?"

"You're lying," Beth said.

"Am I?" he stalked closer. "Maybe I am. Maybe I'm not. But know this: Camdan MacAuley canna be trusted. I learned that to my detriment when that bastard double-crossed me. Giving him a beating was only the beginning of the payment he owes me. Enough talking. Come."

He yanked on the ropes again, pulling her after him. They passed through the courtyard and down a set of spiral steps into some sort of cellar. She was pushed unceremoniously into a damp room full of empty barrels. MacGregor sliced the ropes from her wrists then exited the room, slamming the door shut behind him. Beth pressed herself to the tiny grille in the door.

"He'll come for me you know!" she yelled. "Cam will come."

MacGregor paused and looked back over his shoulder. A wicked smile crossed his face. "Oh, I'm counting on it, lass. I'm counting on it."

With that, the outlaw leader left, his footsteps receding into the distance.

Beth massaged her aching wrists, working some feeling back into them and then tried the door. It was locked, of course. Next, she explored every inch of the room, searching for a way out. There was a boarded up chute in one corner which suggested this was the cellar where the castles victuals were once kept but try as she might, she couldn't get the boards loose. There was no other exit.

With an exasperated growl, she gave up and perched atop one of the empty barrels. They were tall enough that her feet dangled off the ground and she was grateful to be out of the damp muck that covered the floor and away from the rats that no doubt inhabited the place. Her stomach knotted with dread. How the hell was she going to get out of here?

She fumbled in the pocket of her dress and pulled out her cell phone. The battery was almost dead but she flicked it on anyway in the irrational hope that there might be a cell signal. Of course, there wasn't. Oh, what she wouldn't give to be able to call the police right now! Flicking to the camera app, she scrolled through some of the photos stored on it. Her heart twisted as one she'd taken of Cam flashed up. He hadn't known she'd taken it. He was seated on a log by their campfire, blue eyes staring into the distance.

Her heart skipped at the sight. Fear for him made her insides churn. But mixed in with the worry was something else: unease. Had MacGregor been telling the truth?

He has fooled ye as he fools so many.

Cam had never mentioned MacGregor and from his reaction when they first met him on the road, it was obvious the two men knew each other.

Travelers would pay priests to pray for them the night before they set out, hoping that God would spare them the wrath of the Demon Blade. Cam was the most feared brigand of them all.

Could it be true? Surely not? She'd seen first hand how dangerous Cam could be, but that was in the heat of a fight, when he was battling for his life. He would never pray on innocent people.

Would he?

She pressed her hands against her face and took a deep breath as despair welled up and threatened to choke her. Did she know Cam at all?

Chapter 13

Some time later the sound of a key in the lock jolted Beth out of a doze. She was curled into an awkward position atop the barrel but came awake instantly as the door opened. Her cramped muscles screamed as she jerked upright and then jumped down from the barrel, putting her back against it as she faced the door.

A man she didn't recognize stepped inside. Short and nondescript, he had a thatch of greasy, thinning hair hanging around his face. The man looked her over and leered before spitting onto the floor.

"What do you want?" Beth demanded.

"Boss wants to see ye," the man replied. "Ye are to come with me. Would be better for ye if ye do so voluntarily." He shrugged. "But it's all the same to me. Shall we?" He nodded at the open door.

Beth swallowed then crossed to the door. The man came up behind her and she felt the prod of a blade point against her back.

"Dinna try anything stupid."

"Wouldn't dream of it," Beth murmured.

The man guided her back through the castle on the same route she'd used with MacGregor earlier. As they neared the courtyard, she heard the low hum of many voices and as they reached it she saw that the wooden benches were now crammed full of people. The newcomers were all men, some dressed as raggedly as the outlaws, but others wearing fine clothes that marked them out as prosperous merchants or men of some import. They were chatting amongst themselves and an air of excited expectation hung over the space. Over in the corner a man was scrawling numbers onto a large piece of slate and there seemed to be a lot of money changing hands. What the hell was going on?

The crowd noticed Beth's entrance and more than one leer was aimed in her direction but nobody spoke to her as the guard steered her through the crowd to a bench at the back that was raised higher than the others. MacGregor sprawled on the bench, a richly dressed man wearing a plaid pattern she didn't recognize, seated by his side. MacGregor stood and gave her a bow.

"Ah! Glad ye could join us, my lady. Please, take a seat."

Beth perched herself uneasily on the bench. From here she had an unobstructed view of the whole room and she could see over the heads of the crowd to the cage.

"Lady Beth Carter, I'd like ye to meet Alistair Stewart, an associate of mine. He owns the lands that border the mountains. We have an...arrangement."

The richly dressed man scowled at MacGregor. "An arrangement? I would call it more than that. A partnership. I allow you free passage through my lands, risking the wrath of the king should he find out so I expect fully half the takings from this venture, as we agreed!"

"Of course!" MacGregor said, smiling. "As we agreed."

Alistair Stewart turned cold eyes on Beth. "Yer latest doxy, MacGregor?"

MacGregor snorted. "Naught so simple. Lady Carter is my ticket to riches."

"Riches?" Stewart snapped. "What does that mean?"

MacGregor only smiled. "Ye will see." He waved a hand and one of his men hurried over carrying a trencher of roasted meat. MacGregor grabbed a chicken leg and began tearing at it. "Would ye care for something to eat, my lady?"

Beth's stomach growled. In truth she was starving but there was no way she was going to accept any of this snake's hospitality. She didn't answer his question but pointedly looked away. Her defiance seemed to amuse him. He barked a laugh, waved away the serving man, and then climbed to his feet, spreading his arms wide.

A hush settled over the room. All eyes turned towards MacGregor. "Welcome to my kingdom!" he yelled. "As ye can see, the rumors of my demise were greatly exaggerated and I am still very much in business! I am still the humble servant of ye shrewd gentlemen who are here to make themselves rich and have some entertainment into the bargain!" There was a rumble of cheers at this. "Now, let us delay no longer! All wagers have been placed. Let the entertainment begin!"

Two men strode into the courtyard and were let into the cage through a small door. The men were stripped to the waist, their hair pulled into a tight tail at the back of their heads. They were both big, scarred men who were obviously used to fighting. They entered the cage and took up fighting stances three paces apart. Neither were armed but there were weapons tossed in various spots on the floor of the cage. Beth spotted a spear, a sword, a mace.

Her stomach contracted with loathing as she realized what she was witnessing. This was a fighting pit. A place where men came to earn money with their fighting skills and other men came to make money by betting on the winner. Such things still existed in the twenty-first century, despite them being illegal in most civilized countries. But even those she'd heard about during her training as a lawyer didn't allow the use of weapons. The fact that such lethal weapons had been tossed into the arena could only mean one thing: a fight to the death. She suddenly felt nauseous and grabbed the edge of the bench to keep from falling.

MacGregor grinned around at the spectators and then raised his arm above his head, his hand clenched into a fist. Then he brought his arm down in a swift, smooth gesture, signaling the beginning of the bout.

The two men whirled into motion, both splitting away to grab the weapons. One seized a sword, the other a mace, and they began circling like two predators. The crowd burst into a chorus of yelling and whistling, shouting encouragement to whichever of the men they had betted on.

Beth pressed her eyes closed, fighting the nausea that threatened to pitch her from her seat. *No, no, no*, she told herself. *This is not happening. This is a nightmare and I'll wake up in a minute.* But the sounds that came to her from the fighting cage asserted that it was very, very real. She heard the clang of weapons, the grunt of exertion, the horrible wet crunch as weapon met flesh.

A cheer erupted and despite herself, Beth opened her eyes. One of the men lay on the ground, a pool of blood spreading beneath his still form whilst the other stood over him, holding up his sword triumphantly. Beside her, MacGregor was clapping, a wide grin splitting his face. Alistair Stewart scowled and then handed over a fat purse which MacGregor grabbed.

"Ye should have listened to me," he said to his companion. "I told ye ye were betting on the wrong man. Mayhap ye'll listen to my advice for the next bout."

Next bout? Beth thought. *You mean there's more of this madness?* She looked around, desperately searching for a way to escape but she was surrounded by a sea of outlaws, all half-mad with the sight of blood.

A sudden commotion spread through the crowd as they turned to look towards the corridor that lead to the room. Approaching footsteps echoed along its length and then three men stepped inside. Two of them were obviously MacGregor's guardsman but the third was the sight Beth had been praying for.

Cam.

He walked with a slight limp and had a bandage torn from his shirt tied around his thigh but that was the only concession made to his injury. The guards grabbed him, forcing him to halt, and his eyes roved over the gathering, searching. They came to rest on Beth and she felt her breath leave her. The room, the noise, the yowl of the men, all fell away as she met Cam's gaze across the room.

Sudden hope flared in her chest and she surged to her feet, ready to fling herself in his direction, to fight her way through if she had to. But MacGregor's cold fingers suddenly closed around her wrist, as hard as iron.

He stood. A hush fell through the room.

"Welcome!" MacGregor called. "Ye are right on time, my old friend. The second bout is just about to begin. I'm sure our champion, Iain, would like to test his mettle against the Demon Blade."

A murmur went through the room and Beth saw looks of disbelief on the faces of the spectators. The guards flanking Cam suddenly looked wary. They gripped the hilts of their weapons, expecting trouble.

Cam tore his gaze away from Beth, turning to look at MacGregor. "Ye knew I would come."

"Of course. Men like us, we are what we are. Ye canna resist the lure of glory. I knew ye would fight for me! I'll make ye a rich man, my friend!"

Cam nodded. "Aye, I'll fight for ye. But I dinna want yer polluted gold."

"Oh?" MacGregor asked, his grip tightening on Beth's wrist. "What is it ye want?"

Cam pointed at Beth. "Her. If I win, ye let her go. That is my price."

MacGregor grinned. "Done! Well, what do ye think, lads? Who will win? Our new champion or the old? Who's betting on the Demon Blade?"

The room exploded into a cacophony of yelling and arguing. The man chalking up the odds on the piece of slate was suddenly inundated with people clamoring to make new wagers. MacGregor's men stepped into the cage and dragged out the body whilst the champion stared through the bars at Cam.

Through it all Cam stood motionless as the tide of blood-lust washed around him. His face was blank but the eyes that sought out Beth were haunted.

Don't do it, Beth thought. *Don't do it, Cam. Please.*

But when one of MacGregor's men prodded him into the cage, he went. He limped to the center and stood facing his opponent. The new champion crossed his arms, glaring at his challenger. Cam's expression didn't change but his stance shifted slightly, rocking onto the balls of his feet, ready for action.

Beth's heart thundered in her chest hard enough to crack a rib. Cold sweat slid down her spine and her legs could no longer support her. *I have to stop this,* she thought. *I have to.* But she had no way to do that. She was as trapped as Cam in that cage. MacGregor released his grip and she slumped onto the bench, hugging her arms around herself as if cold.

MacGregor raised his arm and silence fell across the crowd. An air of barely contained excitement filled the room, an excitement that sickened Beth. These men wanted to see blood and that blood might very well be Cam's. MacGregor brought his arm swinging down and the contest began.

The champion spun away and grabbed the sword. Cam remained still, his eyes tracking his opponent's movements. The champion came up swinging, gripping the huge sword in a two-handed grip and swinging at Cam's mid-riff hard enough to split him in two. Except Cam wasn't there anymore. At the last instant, he side-stepped, neatly avoiding the swinging blade. The champion grunted, arrested his swing and pivoted, stabbing at Cam's chest. Agile as a snake, Cam swayed out of the way so that the blade went past him.

The fight went on like this for several minutes. Cam made no attempt to pick up a weapon or to engage his opponent, he just dodged out of the way and avoided the champion's attacks. Even with a damaged leg his reflexes were like lightning and no matter what he tried, the champion wasn't able to pin him down.

The crowd began to get restless. They'd come here to see blood spilled, not two men dancing. Boos began to ring around the hall. The champion lost patience.

He stabbed his blade towards Cam's chest, then, as Cam darted away, lashed out with his boot and kicked Cam in his injured thigh. With a cry of pain, the leg gave out and Cam crashed to his knees, blood splattering the floor. The champion saw his chance. He brought his blade swinging towards Cam's unprotected neck, the cold steel glittering in the light from the torches.

Beth surged to her feet. "Cam!" she screamed but her voice was lost amidst the hollering of the spectators.

The blade came singing down and when it was mere millimeters from his skin Cam threw himself to the side and rolled, but not before the blade sliced a red line across his cheek.

He came to his feet. Reaching up, he wiped his hand across his face and stood looking down at his palm for a moment, staring at the blood that covered it. His fingers twitched. His tattoo, Beth noticed, was beginning to glow and when he looked up she saw that look in his eyes again, that look that said all reason had evaporated and he was in the grip of his curse. Rage and blood-lust shone in his eyes.

He grinned. "Well played," he said to his opponent. "But that will be the only mark ye make on me."

He spun and dived to his left, grabbed the spear and held it with hands on either end of the pole, using it like a staff. He slid to one knee and thrust the spear out in front of him, catching the champion's sword on it, mere inches from his face.

The champion pulled his lips back in a snarl of effort. His shoulders strained as he sought to push Cam back, to break his grip and send his blade crunching into his neck. But Cam held. Bracing his injured leg under him, he pushed, his face becoming a mask of pain and effort. With an almighty heave, he shoved the champion back and surged to his feet, the spear clasped in two hands.

Making not a sound, Cam attacked. Using the spear like a staff, he swung at the champion and suddenly he was the one blocking and desperately parrying. Cam moved so fast he was a blur.

A murmur began to go around the gathering and Beth heard the words *Demon Blade* muttered in awe.

Beth perched on the edge of her seat, heart thundering, a growing sense of horror filling her veins. Here was the Camdan MacAuley that MacGregor had told her about. Here was the Cam she'd encountered in the clearing when she'd first fallen through time. This Cam wore a feral grin as he fought and his eyes were alight with mindless blood-lust.

Then suddenly, Cam's spear broke in half with a crunch that echoed through the chamber. The spectators gasped. The champion grinned, thinking he had the advantage. But Cam didn't pause. Unarmed, he head-butted the champion square on the nose. Blood spurted and the champion staggered back, one hand going to his face. With an almost nonchalant ease, Cam smashed the sword from the man's grip with one half of the broken spear and then slammed the hard wooden pole against the man's knee-cap.

The champion screamed and collapsed onto his hands and knees, blood from his broken nose slowly dripping to the floor. Cam bent and grabbed the man's fallen sword, holding it above his neck like an executioner.

The crowd broke into a fit of howling and hollering. "Kill! Kill! Kill!"

"No," Beth whispered. "Don't do it. Please. Don't do it."

As if he heard her words, even though they were drowned in the tumult, Cam suddenly looked up and met her gaze. His expression was ravaged. She could see the war that was raging within him. His arm, where it gripped the sword, was trembling. His curse was calling for fulfilment, calling for blood. Yet Cam resisted. He gritted his teeth and blinked rapidly, the madness fading from his eyes.

He tossed the sword into the dirt and wiped sweat from his forehead with the back of his hand. The room fell silent, the patrons giving each other confused glances.

"It's over," Cam yelled at MacGregor.

MacGregor rose to his feet. "Not yet it isnae! Ye know the rules! Only one man leaves the cage alive. Finish him!"

The crowd took up the chant. "Finish him! Finish him!"

Cam looked round at them with disgust. "Damn yer rules!" he yelled. "This day *two* men leave the cage alive!"

MacGregor's hands curled into fists. His face flushed livid. "If ye willnae finish him then ye forfeit the bout! Iain is declared champion!"

It was a mistake. At his words the room burst into an uproar, those who'd placed bets on Cam rounding on MacGregor with angry shouts and raised fists. Nobody was paying Beth any attention. She seized her chance. She climbed slowly to her feet so as not to alert MacGregor who was busy remonstrating with Alistair Stewart, and shuffled to the edge of the row of benches where an aisle led through to the front of the room.

Once there, she ran. Dodging quickly through the knots of arguing men, she kept low, bent almost double to try and lose herself in the press of waving arms and angry shouting. She skirted along the edge of the room to the cage door.

Cam rushed to it, hands wrapping around the bars. "Beth!" he said hoarsely. "Have they hurt ye?"

"I'm fine," she muttered. "My god, Cam, we have to get out of here!" She grabbed the door and yanked but it was locked.

"Stand back," Cam ordered.

He slammed his shoulder into the door. It sprang open with a crash but the room was in such an uproar that only one or two people noticed and their sudden shouts of alarm went unheard in the hubbub. Cam staggered through the door and grabbed Beth's hand.

"Come on."

Together they hurried into the corridor. Beth's pulse was hammering in her ears and she clung tight to Cam's hand as though it was the only thing that could keep her upright. Two figures came running down the corridor, alerted by the commotion in the fighting pit.

"Hoi!" one of them shouted. "What are ye doing out here?"

They grabbed their weapons but Cam landed a blow to the man's chin that laid him out cold, his sword clattering into the dirt. The second man sprang at Cam's back but Beth grabbed the sword and smacked the flat of the blade into the man's temple. His eyes rolled back in his head, his knees buckled and he collapsed to the floor, rolling around and groaning. Beth dropped the sword from suddenly nerveless fingers.

Cam nodded his thanks then grabbed her hand. Together they pelted across an empty courtyard and then, instead of turning towards the main gate, Cam guided her left, down a set of crumbling stairs to a hole in the wall that led out onto a windswept plateau. Ahead the plateau plunged a hundred feet or more into a ravine below and the ground was slippery and treacherous. The wind snatched at Beth's hair and sent icy fingers under her clothes but after the sweaty gloom of the fighting pit she sucked in the fresh air eagerly.

"This way."

Cam kept a tight hold of her hand as they skirted the edge of the plateau, the rundown curtain wall of the fortress at their backs. Circumventing the wall, they reached the edge of the plateau and stepped out onto a trail that snaked its way downhill into a stand of fir trees. They ran.

Beth dared not look back but any minute she expected to hear the alarm call and then pursuit but all she could hear was the blood roaring in her ears. They slipped and skidded on the muddy trail but dare not slow. Cam ran with this teeth bared, limping on his injured leg, blood seeping from the cut on his face.

"Cam," she said, shuddering to a stop. "Wait a minute. Let me look at those wounds."

"Nay," he replied, shaking his head. "There isnae time."

"But you're bleeding!"

"Do ye think they'll wait politely whilst ye bind it for me? They'll be after us any minute and this time they willnae hesitate to kill me and have their sport with ye."

Beth's blood ran cold. She nodded and they set off again. Beth was relieved when they reached the treeline and the fortress was blocked from view. Cam laboured on but his pace was slowing, his limp becoming more pronounced. How could the man run at all with an arrow wound in his leg?

His curse, she answered herself.

The tattoo was still glowing, his rage thwarted by his refusal to kill the man in the arena. Instead, Cam was channelling the power into pushing his body beyond its limits. How long could he keep it up? His face was pale and his hair stuck to his face in a sweaty tangle, his teeth bared in pain.

She curled her fingers around his. "Lean on me. Take some of the weight off that leg."

He glanced at her and she thought he would argue but he only nodded. Beth pulled his arm across her shoulder and wrapped her arm around his waist, and like this they struggled down the trail.

Cam grimaced in pain at each step but made not a sound. All the while Beth listened for the crash of pursuit, her ears straining to pick out the shouts of men and the pounding of feet. Ahead, the trail levelled out and they suddenly found themselves standing on the banks of a wide river. The water ran high and fast, milky white with run off from the mountains. Its hiss and gurgle filled the air, far more violent than the river she and Cam had fished in only yesterday. Lord, had it only been a day? So much had changed in so short a time.

Cam pushed away from Beth's support and staggered down to the river's edge. He leaned over, scanning the turbulent water and then glanced back up at the trail. His expression tightened.

"They're coming."

Beth strained her ears and then she heard it: the baying of dogs in the distance. Her blood ran cold. With Cam's injured leg there was no way they could outrun them. His expression turned determined. He held out his hand to her.

"There's only one way," he said. "We have to go into the river."

Her eyes widened. "Into that? Are you crazy? We'll drown!"

"Nay, we willnae," he replied. "I'll keep ye safe." He was still holding out his hand. His blue eyes fixed on hers. "Beth, do ye trust me?"

AT HIS QUESTION, BETH hesitated. A shadow of uncertainty filled her eyes. The sight of it cut Cam to the bone. When she looked at him her expression wasn't filled with the bright hope it had only yesterday. Now it was filled with uncertainty, mistrust. It would have hurt less if she'd have taken a knife to his heart.

Steeling himself, Cam met her gaze and said again. "There isnae another way, lass. They'll be here in moments."

She glanced up at the trail to where the sound of baying dogs was getting closer. Then she looked at Cam and pulled in a deep breath. "I trust you."

She grasped his hand, came to stand by his side. He nodded at her.

"Jump when I say. Ready?"

She bit her lip and nodded. Lord, but she was the bravest woman he'd ever met.

"Now!"

Together they launched themselves from the bank. Cam kept a firm grip of Beth's hand as they hit the water and the cold tried to snatch away his breath and pull him under. He didn't let it. Despite the weakness in his right thigh, he forced his legs to kick, to propel him to the surface, dragging Beth with him. They broke the surface and gulped in air, fighting to keep their heads above the swirling maelstrom.

Cam pulled Beth close to him, got one arm around her and swam with the other, kicking powerfully beneath them. The rage of his curse had not abated, it still swirled in his blood like fire but now he channelled it into his limbs, used every ounce of his will to force it to do his bidding, to give him the strength he needed to keep them both alive in this vortex of swirling, grasping, freezing water.

The current was stronger than he expected. It grabbed them, sent them hurtling along with the speed of a galloping horse. Flotsam zoomed past: broken branches, mats of reeds and other detritus that had been washed from higher in the mountains.

Beth clung tight to him, her face pale, gulping in breaths and doing her best to swim with the current. A log slammed into Cam's shoulder and pain lanced through him, sending his vision white. His grip on Beth slipped and she was torn from his grasp, swept away by the swirling water.

"Beth!" he bellowed.

With an almighty kick, he sped after her. He'd always been a strong swimmer and had spent many hours in the river near Dun Ringill with his brothers. Now he needed every ounce of strength and skill he'd learned under his father's tutelage. With strong, powerful strokes, he cut through the water, ignoring the burning in his legs, the weakness where blood leaked from the arrow wound. Beth needed him. He would not give up.

She bobbed ahead of him, fighting to keep her head above the water. She was beginning to tire. Cam knew first hand how quickly the freezing water leeched strength from limbs and unlike him, Beth was unused to the cold of the Highlands. Moment by moment her movements were becoming slower, her head dipping that little bit closer to the water's turbulent surface.

Damn ye! Cam growled at himself. *Faster! Ye willnae fail her now!*

His lungs were burning and his heart was hammering so hard in his chest that he felt it thundering against his ribs. Still he pushed himself harder. His outstretched fingers brushed the sleeve of her dress for a moment before she was ripped out of his reach once more. He propelled himself after her, his arms pumping, his legs kicking. At last he came within reach and this time his fingers closed around her wrist and he pulled her to him. He held her tight around the waist, boosting her so that her head was well clear of the foaming swell.

With a sob, she threw her arms around his shoulders, clinging to him tightly.

"I've got ye," he called above the tumult of the water. "I've got ye."

Glancing behind, Cam saw a log come speeding towards them. As it rushed past he reached out and snared it, dragging it closer. It was thick enough to bear their weight so Cam supported Beth whilst she threw an arm across it and then followed her example, all the while keeping one arm clamped around her waist. He'd lost her once. He wouldn't risk it again.

Like this, clinging to the floating log, they were carried along by the river, tossed and turned like two pieces of flotsam. The pain in Cam's thigh was throbbing like fire and now the muscles in his arms were cramping from holding Beth with one and the log with the other. But he wouldn't let go.

I willnae fail her, he said to himself over and over again. *I willnae fail.*

His body alight with agony, his promise to Beth the only thing that kept him focused, Cam lost all sense of time. He couldn't have said how long they were in the river. It could have been only a heartbeat or an eternity but finally, blessedly, the river began to widen and its flow to ease. The churning white water calmed to a glassy serenity, flowing languidly between broad, mossy banks.

The current swept them towards the western shore and when they were close enough, Cam gripped Beth tightly, kicked away from the log, and swam for shore. Next to him Beth moved feebly but her eyes kept drifting closed.

Alarm spiked through him and he kicked harder, desperation and panic adding strength to his exhausted muscles. Finally he felt his feet touch the bottom and he dragged Beth, semi-conscious, through the shallows, up the shore and onto the grassy sward beyond.

Laying her gently on her back, he leaned over and shook her. "Beth? Beth, lass, wake up. We've made it. We're clear of the river."

Beth's eyelids fluttered and she muttered something but didn't stir. Her skin was deathly pale and, placing the palm of his hand against her cheek, he realized she was freezing. Warmth. She needed warmth, and fast.

With an effort of will Cam pushed his battered body to its feet and stumbled into the treeline, searching for firewood. They had been fortunate that it hadn't rained in a while—a rare occurrence in these parts—and so there was plenty of dry, fallen wood littering the forest floor. He gathered an armload and hurried back to Beth.

Dumping it to the ground, he arranged it as he'd been taught as a child, with kindling first and bigger sticks ready to feed into it once the blaze was going. He'd lost his saddlebags when MacGregor had taken Firefly and with them, his flint and tinder. He would have to start a fire the hard way. Taking a dry stick he placed it into a notch on another stick and began spinning it between his palms, trying to work up enough friction to light a spark.

It was slow, gruelling work and he soon had blisters to add to his mounting list of injuries. He ignored them. He could not stop. Not until Beth was safe. His teeth bared in a snarl of determination, he kept at it, flicking his head back from time to time to stop his wet hair dripping onto his handiwork. He kept glancing at Beth but she lay as still as a waxwork doll. Only her shallow breathing showed that she still lived.

Finally a wisp of smoke began to rise from the wood and Cam carefully blew on it, feeding in tiny bits of kindling—a difficult task with fingers that felt as useless as sausages—until a flame took. The heat, after the cold of the river, felt wonderful but he couldn't rest yet.

He knelt next to Beth. She didn't stir but her eyelids fluttered as though she was dreaming. Her skin felt deathly cold and there was a slight blue tinge to her lips.

"Wake up, lass," he said, shaking her. "Ye need to get warm."

No reaction. Cam rocked back on his heels, thinking. She would not warm whilst she was in those wet clothes. Making a decision, he stripped off his plaid and shirt and laid them out by the fire to dry. Then he quickly unlaced Beth's dress and wrestled her out of it. She didn't respond as he peeled the heavy, wet garment away and laid it out next to his plaid by the fire. Leaving Beth in only her under shift, Cam lifted her into his arms. He carried her over to the fire and sat down with his back against a rock, Beth leaning against his naked chest. He rubbed her arms vigorously and then wrapped his arms around her, trusting the flames and his own body heat to warm her.

Cam drew a great, deep breath through his nostrils and let it out slowly. Safe. They were safe—for now at least. He looked around, trying to figure out where they were. He didn't recognise their immediate surroundings but judging from the position of the sun the river had carried them west—far to the west unless he missed his guess.

Frowning, he squinted into the distance. Along the horizon marched a low line of hills covered in purple heather with a flat expanse of floodplain before them. In the middle of the floodplain winked a loch in the distinctive shape of a tear drop.

Cam's stomach tightened as realization dawned on him. He knew where he was all right. These lands were ones he'd wandered for most of his life. The river had spat them out right on the border of MacAuley lands. On the other side of those hills lay Dun Ringill, his childhood home.

He hadn't set foot on those lands for many years, not since the night his curse had taken him. Involuntarily, he glanced at his tattoo. The markings were pale now, little more than a shadow on his skin. But for how long? How long till the rage came roaring back, turning him into a mindless beast? He squeezed his eyes shut against a sudden pain that twisted his soul. A mindless beast. Was that what Beth thought him now? The look of mistrust in her eyes haunted him.

In MacGregor's hide-out she'd discovered what he really was. Not a good man weighed down by the weight of circumstances beyond his control. Not an honorable man trying his best to keep to the code taught to him by his father. Nay, he was none of these things. He was a fighter. A killer. How could he have forgotten that? He'd done too much to ever hope for redemption.

He glanced again at those hills. His home was so near. Was it coincidence that had brought him this close? Was it pure chance that put him within touching distance of his old life? Within touching distance of the brother who'd somehow managed to break his own curse? It was less than a day's walk to Dun Ringill. He and Beth could be there by sundown tomorrow.

It's too late, he thought. I've done too much, seen too much to ever go back. The real Camdan MacAuley was the man in the fighting pit, the one Beth looked at with such doubt. Better that she is free of me. Better that they're all free of me.

He grabbed his shirt and stuck his finger into the pocket, relieved when his finger brushed something hard. Drawing it out, Cam hefted a small leather pouch that contained his money, along with one other important keepsake, the only thing he hadn't lost when MacGregor took Firefly. Now that his horse was gone, the last connection to his old life had gone too. He hoped MacGregor would treat the stallion well.

The coins inside clinked as he opened the purse and peered inside. And then it came to him. He knew what he had to do. He brushed a strand of hair from Beth's face.

"I love ye," he whispered to her softly, even though he knew she couldn't hear. "More than ye will ever know."

He'd made a promise and he would keep it. He'd ensure Beth got home safely, even if it tore out his heart.

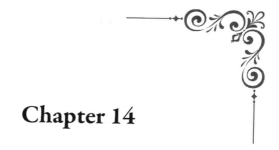

Chapter 14

Beth was cold. Even the roaring fire burning in the fireplace could do nothing to chase out the chill that seemed to seep into her bones. Hugging her arms around herself, she glanced at the clock above the mantelpiece. Almost 10.30. She hoped her parents were having a good time at the theater. They'd soon be home to tell her all about it. She shifted uneasily, the sofa creaking beneath her. Her parents? She ought to remember something about them, something important. She shivered. This didn't feel right. Something was wrong.

A knock on the door made her jump, spilling the TV remote onto the carpet. She jumped to her feet and hurried into the hall. Who would be calling at this hour of the night?

She pulled the door open and a frigid blast of the cold January air sent goose bumps riding up her skin. Two police officers stood on the veranda. Something about their expressions sent a chill down her spine. She hugged herself tighter.

"We need you to come with us, Miss," said one. "There's something you need to see."

She followed them to the squad car and sat in silence whilst they drove her somewhere. They pulled up and one of them looked at her expectantly.

"We're here."

Through the window she could see nothing but darkness. "Where?"

"You'll see. Go inside."

Beth stepped out of the car and suddenly she was back in MacGregor's hideout. Before her stood the fighting cage and she was sat on one of the benches, watching. She was the only spectator. Inside the cage two men fought but she couldn't make out their faces.

The bench creaked and she turned to see an old woman take a seat next to her. She had iron-gray hair pulled back in a bun and dark eyes like pools of ink.

Beth blinked. "Irene?"

The old woman smiled. "Were ye expecting somebody else?"

Beth stared at her for a moment. "I'm dreaming aren't I?"

"Aye, lass," Irene said with a nod.

Beth turned to watch the fight. Now she could make out the men's faces and realized they were the same person: Cam. He fought himself.

"Why are you showing me this?" Beth demanded.

"I?" Irene said. "I am showing ye naught. This is yer dream, Bethany Carter."

The two Cams were circling each other, weapons held ready. Sweat covered each of them, along with a hundred minor wounds that were slowly dripping blood onto the floor. One of the men stood tall while the other crouched. One had a feral snarl on his face whilst the other had eyes full of sorrow. One had a blazing white brand on his arm, the other only a faint tracery of a pattern. But they were both Cam. The different sides of himself, endlessly at war.

"Who are ye going to place a wager on?" Irene asked. "Who do ye want to win? The good man or the bad?"

"Neither," Beth replied, realizing it was true. "They're both Cam. Without either, he wouldn't be the man he is."

Irene lifted an eyebrow. "Only a few short weeks ago ye wouldnae have said so. Ye would have condemned a man like Camdan MacAuley."

"Yes," Beth said. "I would." She glanced down at the two men circling each other. "But I guess I've grown up. The world was neat and ordered when I could separate it up nicely: the good guys and the bad guys. I guess now I realize it doesn't work that way." She turned to look at Irene. "We're the sum of our experiences," she said, thinking back on how the loss of her parents had sent her running from her homeland and how it took a man she would once have dismissed as a thug to set her free of that pain. "And I guess I've come to realize there is always a different path to tread."

Irene smiled, her eyes alight with delight. "Aye, lass. There is. What choice will ye make now?"

"I've already made it."

Irene and the fighting pit disappeared and warmth suddenly enveloped her. Something had a hold of her, something hard and solid and wholly reassuring. She knew it would never let her go. It would always keep her safe.

She opened her eyes slowly, blinking in the light. A few feet away a fire blazed merrily, sending out delicious tendrils of heat to caress her skin, chasing away the last of the freezing darkness. The warm, reassuring presence at her back remained and strong arms were wrapped around her. After a moment she realized she was leaning against Cam, his chest pressing into her back, his arms curled protectively around her middle.

For a moment she did nothing. She sat there, experiencing the simple pleasure of being so close to him, his smell filling her nostrils, his breathing soft and gentle by her ear, his skin warm against hers.

Yes, she thought. *I've already made my choice.*

He was asleep. His head had fallen back against the rock he leaned on and his eyes were closed. Red-gold hair lay in damp tangles across his shoulders and the dunking in the river had cleaned the cut on his cheek, leaving a neat red line across his cheekbone. He seemed so peaceful, all his cares gone, so different to the man who'd stepped into the fighting pit.

She gently traced her finger tips down the length of his arm.

He stirred, his eyes fluttering open. "Beth!" he exclaimed. "Ye are awake! How do ye feel?"

"I'm well. Thanks to you." She gazed at him. "I knew you'd come for me."

"Of course I'd come for ye," he replied. "Ye think I would leave ye to face it without me? After causing ye such hardship?" His voice was bitter, full of self-recrimination.

Beth shook her head. "It wasn't your fault they attacked us. How were you to know they were hiding out in the mountains?"

His eyes were full of old pain as he shook his head. "It *was* my fault, lass. Of course it was. Ye wouldnae have been in that position if it wasnae for me. I'm sorry. For everything. What ye saw in that place...what I did..." He broke off.

"Was he telling the truth?" Beth asked, forcing out the words. She had to know. "Were you and MacGregor partners?"

Did you used to terrorize people like he said? Oh god, Cam, tell me you didn't!

He didn't answer for a long time as if he was thinking through his answer. But finally he shook his head and Beth let out a breath she hadn't known she'd been holding.

"MacGregor has no partners. I used to fight for him, that's all. It was an easy way to make money. I left. I thought I wasnae that man anymore. I didnae want ye to see that. If I had listened to Rabbie's warning we wouldnae be in this mess. I'm sorry."

Beth pressed a finger against his lips. "It's no good dwelling on 'what ifs'. We're both safe now. That's all that matters."

"Is it?" he asked hoarsely.

Beth didn't like the haunted look in his eyes. "Come on," she said, scooting over to where their clothes were laid out near the fire. "As much as I could happily sit here staring at your chest all day, the fire's dying down and it's getting chilly."

He didn't smile at her attempt at humor as he took his plaid and pulled it on. Beth yanked the dress over her head, wriggled into it, and tied up the laces. It was blessedly warm and dry although her boots were still damp.

Cam pushed himself stiffly to his feet, a grimace of pain baring his teeth as he put weight on his injured leg.

"That needs looking at," Beth said, pointing at the rock. "Sit."

"'Tis fine," he muttered. "Dinna worry yerself."

Beth crossed her arms and raised one eyebrow. "Sit."

He frowned and reluctantly did as she asked. Beth hiked up the kilt of his plaid to reveal the smooth skin of his thigh. The arrow wound formed a ragged puncture halfway between his knee and groin. It looked to have torn the meat of the muscle but hadn't penetrated deeply enough to become embedded or to hit any major arteries, thank goodness. A large purple bruise surrounded the puncture and he'd torn open the scab so it was bleeding again, a bright rivulet running down his leg.

Beth swore under her breath. How had he managed to keep them both afloat with such an injury, much less drag her to shore and then build a fire? It must be agony. Yet Cam brushed off the pain as though it was no more than an annoying insect.

"You need to see a doctor," she said. "Or whatever passes for that in your time. It needs stitching and something to keep out the infection."

He smiled wryly. "Do ye see any such thing around here?"

She huffed out a breath, conceding the point. "All right. I'll bandage it as best I can but we find the nearest place with a doctor and get you looked at, agreed?"

"As ye say."

Beth bent and tore the hem off the bottom of her dress. Kneeling, she wound it around his wounded leg, bandaging it tight. Cam grimaced in pain but made not a sound.

"Where do you reckon we are?" she asked him. "Do you think MacGregor will find us?"

"Nay, lass," Cam replied softly. "We're many miles from his territory. The river carried us right out of the mountains." He looked up, his eyes fixing on a line of hills in the distance. "He wouldnae dare come here," he added, his voice barely above a whisper. "He knows who would oppose him."

Beth finished tying the bandage then stepped back. "There. It should stop the bleeding at least. Hold on a minute." She hurried in amongst the trees and returned holding a stout branch almost as tall as she was which she held out to him. "Here. A walking stick. You can't put too much weight on that leg or you'll aggravate your wound."

He took it gingerly. "My thanks."

Cam clasped the stick in one hand and began limping away from her. Beth watched him go for a moment, wondering what words she could say to make things right between them, to break through his guilt and self-recrimination. With a sigh, she trotted to catch up with him, quickly leaving their makeshift campsite behind.

CAM LED BETH ALONG the river for a while, keeping it on their right as they moved out of the foothills. What had once been a raging white torrent that had done its best to drown them had now become wide and placid, the kind of river that couples would go boating on. Who would have thought how ferociously it raged further upriver? The gray autumn sky reflected in its surface and it was so clear that Beth saw river weed waving languidly in its current.

But when the river tumbled down a series of short waterfalls and then turned towards the sea, Cam veered away and began trudging towards the flood plain in the distance.

"Where are we going?" Beth asked.

Cam glanced at her. He'd said not a word since they'd left their make-shift campsite. "Ye will see," was the only answer he gave.

They walked for over an hour before Cam suddenly halted and gazed out over the plain below. Beth spotted something long and white snaking its way through the purple heather.

"What's that? Another river?"

"Nay," he answered quietly. "It's the Edinburgh road."

Beth's stomach tightened. The Edinburgh road! The road that would take her home.

Home? she thought to herself. *I don't even know where that is anymore.*

When they were only a hundred yards or so from the line of the road, Cam led Beth behind a large group of boulders, hiding them from sight.

"What's wrong?" Beth asked. "You're making me nervous."

Cam tilted his head, holding up a hand for quiet. "Somebody's coming."

Beth froze, a thrill of fear going through her. Could it be MacGregor? Could he have found them after all? She strained her ears and caught the sound of many booted feet. It was interspersed with the creak of wagon wheels. She breathed out slowly. Surely MacGregor wouldn't make so much noise?

Carefully, Beth peered around the outcrop. A long column of people were snaking their way down the road. In the center trundled wagons piled high with goods. Mounted warriors wearing a plaid similar to Cam's guarded the perimeter, keeping pace with the wagons. At the head of the column rode a fat, richly dressed man flanked by two guards.

Cam let out a breath. "Merchant caravan. Wait here while I go and talk to them."

"I'll come with you."

He shook his head. "Nay, ye willnae. Not until I'm sure they're friendly. Stay here, I willnae be long."

Before she could say another word, he broke cover and began limping towards the column. The guards spotted him immediately. Spurring their horses forward, they blocked his path. A conversation followed which Beth couldn't hear and then the guards turned their mounts and escorted Cam back to the fat man.

Beth cursed the distance between them. She couldn't make out a word of what was said but Cam was gesticulating and pointing at the rock Beth crouched behind.

The fat man listened, rubbing his chin, and then nodded. He dismounted and Cam led him back to Beth's hiding place.

"It's all right, lass," he called. "Ye can come out now."

Beth frowned. A prickle of unease walked down her spine. She didn't like this. Something felt wrong. Warily, she edged out into the open, eyeing the fat man cautiously.

"Lady Carter, this is Duncan MacConnell of Clan Mac-Connell," Cam said by way of introduction. "His family and the MacAuleys have been allies for generations."

Beth looked at Cam sharply. *Lady Carter?* Why the hell had he called her that?

The fat man gave her a flourishing bow. "At yer service, my lady. Yer servant here has told me of yer predicament and ye have my sympathy. I canna imagine how unsettling it must be to be captured by vagabonds and carried so far from home."

Beth glanced at Cam, wondering exactly what he'd told this man. Her servant? Captured by vagabonds? Cam watched her steadily and something about his expression warned her to keep up the pretence.

"I...um...yes," she stammered. "Very unsettling."

Duncan MacConnell hooked his thumbs into his belt. "Well, I'm honored to offer ye passage with us."

"Passage?" she asked, confused. "What are you talking about?"

"Lady Carter," Cam said in a low voice. "Duncan is a merchant. His caravan is going to Edinburgh. He's agreed to escort ye there."

Beth stared at him. What? Had she just heard that right?

Duncan MacConnell filled the silence. "Aye, my lady. It would be an honor. I've just come from Dun Ringill, having concluded by trade with Laird MacAuley. The MacAuley wool will fetch a mighty price in Edinburgh ."

Beth frowned. Dun Ringill? Laird MacAuley? What was he talking about? Surely they weren't that close to MacAuley lands? She looked sharply at Cam but he didn't meet her gaze, instead staring at the ground.

"Mr MacConnell," she said, taking a deep breath, "would you mind giving us a moment? I need to have a word with my 'servant' here."

Duncan MacConnell looked uncertainly between Cam and Beth. Then he bowed. "Of course, my lady. I will await yer pleasure." He walked back towards the caravan.

As soon as he was out of earshot Cam held up a hand. "Dinna," he said. "Dinna do this."

"Do what?" Beth snapped. "Demand to know just what the hell you're playing at? What's going on, Cam? Why have you asked that guy to take me to Edinburgh?"

Cam looked up slowly, met her furious gaze. "Because I made a promise to see ye safely there. The MacConnells can be trusted. They're my family's closest allies. Duncan will get ye there safely."

Beth opened her mouth and closed it again. As the full import of his words sank in, a cold hand seemed to reach into her chest and squeeze her heart. "But...but...you mean you aren't coming with me?"

"Nay, lass."

For a moment she was stunned speechless. Never had she contemplated going there without him. He'd been by her side since the moment she'd arrived in this time. Being without him now was unthinkable.

"You're abandoning me? After all we've been through?"

"Abandoning ye?" he replied incredulously. "Canna ye see I'm trying to keep my promise? This is the only way."

"Only way?" she cried incredulously. Her voice rose in pitch as her anger flared. "Only way to do what?"

"To keep ye safe," he responded, anger flaring in his tone as well now. "Lord above, woman, surely ye understand that?"

"Are you kidding me? How will sending me away from you keep me safe?"

"Because *I'm* the danger!" he snapped. "*I'm* the reason ye were taken by MacGregor and his men. *I'm* the reason ye nearly drowned in that river! Me!"

"And you're also the reason I'm still breathing!" she yelled. "You're the reason I didn't get lost in the wilderness when I first arrived or assaulted by those thugs! You're the reason I still have hope of sorting this mess out!"

And you're the reason I feel alive for the first time in my life, she thought.

"Ye could have *died*, Beth!" he said. "And it would have been my fault. I canna risk that again. I willnae. I made a promise to keep ye safe and I will—no matter what that takes."

"And everything that's happened between us? You'll just forget it?"

"Forget it?" he said disbelievingly. He grabbed her arms, gripping them painfully. "Lord, woman, how could ye think such a thing? I thank the Lord for every moment I've spent with ye!"

"Then don't send me away!" she hated the catch in her voice. "Damn you, Camdan! Don't pretend you don't know what's happening to us! What we are becoming to each other!"

He stared at her for a long moment, conflicting emotions warring in his eyes. Then he shook his head. "Aye, I know. But it was an illusion," he breathed, his voice full of pain. "A dream. And now the dream is over. Such things are not meant for men like me. Ye saw what I am: what I *really* am. A fighter. A killer. What do I have to offer ye? Naught but blood and ashes and I willnae allow ye to be dragged into my world. I am cursed Beth."

Beth broke free of his grip and crossed her arms, glaring up at him. "Your brother defeated his curse. Why can't you?"

He shook his head. "It's too late. There isnae a way back for me. Not after all I've done."

"I won't go. I refuse," Beth said.

Cam scrubbed a hand through his hair. "Lord help me, woman, but ye are the most stubborn creature I've ever met. Ye will go with MacConnell, if I have to tie you up and hoist ye into the wagon myself!"

"I'd like to see you try!"

They glared at each other. Hot fury pounded through Beth's veins. How dare he do this to her? Who did he think he was to decide her fate? But underneath the fury grew a cold, hard fear. She couldn't lose him. She couldn't. She had to make him see, make him understand that he wasn't the man he thought he was.

In a softer voice she said, "Cam, listen to me—"

He held up a hand. "Nay, dinna say aught else." The fury was gone from his voice and now it was only filled with pain and longing. He met her gaze and his eyes were ravaged. "Go with the MacConnell. Find a way home. Be safe. Be happy. Please." His words were barely above a whisper and the despair in his voice broke her heart.

He took her hand and gently kissed the back of it. Then, without another word, he turned and began limping away.

Beth stood there, watching him go, feeling her heart slowly crack in half. She ought to run after him. She ought to yell and plead and explain until the fool man understood. But she didn't move. That look in his eyes...

Oh god. Oh god. I'm losing him. The thought exploded through her brain like a gunshot.

Nothing she could say would overcome his self-loathing. Nothing she could do would make him see the man that she saw. And Beth understood, finally, the full impact of his curse. It obliterated everything he'd ever believed about himself, turning him into something he hated. The cruelty of such a fate took her breath away.

Oh, Cam.

She watched him go, tears leaking from the corner of her eyes until he disappeared behind a fold in the land.

She heard a polite cough beside her. Quickly dashing the tears away, she turned to find the merchant, Duncan Mac-Connell, standing there.

"My lady. Time is getting away from us. We must be on our way."

Beth glanced down at her hand and realized she was holding something. Cam must have slipped it into her hand when he kissed it farewell. Uncurling her fingers, she realized it was her parents' pendant, the one she'd given Cam in order to buy their supplies during their stop in Netherlay. He'd never sold it after all.

She glanced up again, trying to catch one last glimpse of him, but he'd disappeared, swallowed by the endless expanse of the Highlands. Taking a deep breath, she slowly closed her hand over the pendant and glanced towards the line of hills that marched along the horizon, marking the border of MacAuley lands.

"Mr MacConnell," she said, making her voice haughty and commanding, the voice of a noblewoman. "I thank you for your assistance. Tell your men to turn the caravan around."

Duncan MacConnell frowned at her. "Turn it around? Whatever for? I've been paid to take ye to Edinburgh, my lady, and that lies to the east."

Beth held her hand up between them allowing the golden pendant to dangle in front of MacConnell's face. "I trust this will be payment enough for you to take me wherever I damn well like?"

The slight widening of MacConnell's eyes told her she'd guessed rightly. "Aye, my lady. I think it might."

"Good. Do as I say. Turn your men around. We aren't going east. We're going west."

Chapter 15

Cam walked and walked and walked. He had no idea where he was going and paid no attention to his surroundings. The pain from his leg wound was a dull, burning ache that pulsed in time with his beating heart. Cam ignored it. Compared to the pain in his soul, it was nothing.

With each step, memories of Beth's face flared in his mind. She'd looked so hurt. So betrayed. Why couldn't she understand? She would be on her way to Edinburgh by now and a way home. It was the only thing he could do for her. It was for the best.

Really? he asked himself bitterly. *Then why does it feel like ye've stabbed yerself in the gut?*

He had to let her go. If he didn't, she was doomed to a life of misery with him, and he would endure any pain, no matter how great, to ensure that didn't happen. So he walked, trying to outrun the burning in his soul. Trying to forget.

He lost all track of time. The sun rose to its zenith and then started to fall towards evening. Cam didn't stop. Hunger gnawed at his belly, thirst tugged at his throat. He didn't stop. Gripping the staff tightly, he limped on, barely noticing when the rutted road under his boots ended and was replaced by wilder, untamed terrain.

It was only when the wind changed direction, bringing with it the scent of the sea and the crash of waves, that Cam finally struggled to a halt and looked around him. He didn't know how far he'd walked but the sun was low in the sky and the place where he'd parted with Beth was a long, long way behind him.

Turning into the wind, he squinted and his stomach clenched at the sight that greeted him.

Ahead of him the gray, rolling ocean spread out to the horizon and white breakers crashed onto the shore less than a hundred meters from where he stood. But that wasn't the sight that sent cold fear clutching at his heart.

Only a few paces in front of him a ring of standing stones rose out of the earth like the dark claws of some grasping, monstrous beast. The light of the setting sun didn't seem to touch them at all and they stood black and unforgiving against the gray of the sea.

Cam's heart thudded as he realized where his treacherous feet had brought him. The Stones of Druach. Where it all began. Where he'd stood with his brothers and made his bargain. Fate, it seemed, had brought him full circle.

Mirth suddenly bubbled up inside him and a hysterical laugh burst from his throat.

"Ha!" he yelled at the stones. "Well met! A fine trick!" Spreading his arms wide he stumbled into the center of the ring and turned in a slow circle. "Well, here I am!" he yelled. "Isnae this what ye desired? What are ye waiting for? Ye wanted my life? Here it is! Take it, damn ye!"

His shout faded into silence, swallowed by the wind and the sighing of the sea. There was no reply. Cam crashed to his knees. Of course, there wouldn't be an answer. The Fae had already taken everything. They'd wanted his life, but that hadn't meant death. No honorable end in battle, fighting to save his clan. Oh no. That would have been too neat. Too easy. They'd desired something far worse.

And they've got it, Cam thought. *I canna do this anymore. It's over.*

A sudden pain seared through his arm. The tattoo—the mark of the Fae—was glowing white hot. This close to the Stones of Druach, the place that gave it birth, the power of his curse was all-consuming. The rage flashed through his blood like magma, bringing with it unbearable pain and a desire for violence that almost wiped away his reason.

Cam clung onto his thoughts, resisted its pull. He would not give in. He would not become a mad man. Not again. Not ever.

With a howl of pain, he collapsed onto his back, wrapping his arms around himself and gritting his teeth as the searing agony rampaged through his body. He convulsed, his legs thrashing against the ground, his fingernails digging into his palms hard enough to draw blood.

Let go, his curse whispered to him. *Give in. All ye have to do is kill and the pain will go away. Why fight it?*

Because I choose to, he answered himself. *Because I willnae be that man ever again.*

He realized suddenly that Irene MacAskill was right. There *was* another path he could choose. It had always been open to him, had he the courage to take it. All he had to do was let his curse consume him.

Lying on his back inside the stone circle, Cam stared up at the sky as it slowly began to darken. Stars lit the night and then the moon rose, bathing the landscape in silver. Cam barely saw it. Blinding agony ripped through him. It felt as though hot daggers were being stabbed into his organs. It felt as though the skin was being flayed from his bones.

Kill! Kill! Kill! screamed the rage.

Cam gritted his teeth and endured the pain. He brought images of Beth to mind. Her smile, her laugh, the way her skin felt under his touch, the indescribable feeling of completeness as he made love to her.

"Beth," he whispered to the darkening sky. "Forgive me."

It would not be long now. He could sense the reserves of his body weakening. As his curse raged through him, it was slowly draining him, burning away his life energy. He drew a deep, agonizing breath and waited to die.

But suddenly he heard movement, the sound of approaching footsteps. Instinct sent him staggering to his feet, hand grasping for a sword that was no longer there.

"Who is it?" he rasped, his voice a hollow croak. "Who's there?"

A voice answered from the darkness. "It's me, Camdan."

A man stepped into the moonlight. He was taller than Cam, and broad-shouldered from long hours working at the forge. Dark hair like their father's framed a stern face and serious eyes.

"It's me," said Logan MacAuley. "I've come to bring ye home, little brother."

BETH WATCHED IN STRICKEN silence as Cam rose to his feet and faced his brother. All the blood drained from his face, leaving him deathly pale. In the moonlight his blue eyes looked like chips of ice.

She crouched in the shadows outside the stone circle with Thea, Logan's wife, a woman who, it turned out to Beth's total shock, was a time traveler like herself.

Duncan MacConnell had delivered Beth to Dun Ringill in the early afternoon and the laird and his wife had seen her immediately after she told the guards why she was there. Logan, a slightly older, dark-haired version of Cam, had listened intently as Beth gabbled, letting her words flood out in a deluge, no longer caring whether he thought her story of time-travel the ramblings of a mad woman.

But he didn't think that. He had risen from his chair and led Beth and Thea to the stables where he'd ordered horses saddled. A brief argument between the laird and his wife followed. Logan wanted her to stay behind, citing her obvious pregnancy as a reason, but Thea, it seemed was just as formidable as her husband, and she'd got her own way in the end.

The three of them had thundered out the gates of Dun Ringill and back to the place where Beth last saw Cam. He was long gone, of course, but Logan was an expert tracker and they'd followed his trail all afternoon, riding the horses into exhaustion to catch up with him.

Now, Beth crouched with Thea and watched as Logan approached his brother, moving slowly as though Cam was a wild animal that might bolt at any minute. Cam's tattoo was blazing and his blond hair was plastered to his head with sweat. Dark shadows filled the hollows under his eyes and the contours of his cheekbones. He stood rigidly, staring at his brother with eyes full of wary disbelief.

Beth's heart broke at the sight of him. She had to help him! She tried to rise to her feet but Thea caught her and pulled her back.

"No," she whispered urgently. "We mustn't interfere. This is between them. Wait and watch."

Beth drew in a ragged breath and nodded.

CAM STARED AT THE APPARITION in front of him. It looked like his brother. Lord above, it even *sounded* like his brother. He looked a little older maybe, but in all other respects Logan looked exactly as he had when they'd parted on that dark night all those years ago.

But it couldn't be.

Cam threw back his head and laughed, his mirth slicing the air like a knife. "Ah! What will ye throw at me next? My mother? My father? Will ye never tire of tormenting me?"

The apparition of Logan spread its hands wide and took a step closer. The dark eyes reflected the moonlight and they were fixed right on Cam, as stern and serious as Cam remembered.

"I'm nay here to torment ye," Logan said, his voice a low rumble in the night. "And this isnae a trick. It's me, Logan. I canna believe I've found ye after all these years. I've come to take ye home."

Cam hesitated. Could it really be him? Logan wore the MacAuley plaid like Cam, but Logan's was clean and made from a rich fabric. The laird's sash was tied diagonally across his chest and their father's sword hung from his hip.

"Do ye think me a fool?" Cam growled, flexing his fingers as the rage surged in him. "Do ye think I would fall for yer tricks? There isnae a way home for me. I agreed to that bargain, remember? I stood in this very circle and traded it away."

Logan shook his head. "Ye are wrong, brother. There is always a way back. Or how else could I be here? I was cursed too, remember? Cursed so that everyone forgot who I was and anyone who stayed close to me would die. Yet here I am."

Cam sucked in a breath. His fingers clenched into fists and he pulled his lips back from his teeth in a snarl. "What are ye talking about?"

Logan took another step. He was careful, Cam noticed, not to make any sudden movements and to keep his hand away from his weapon.

"I thought as ye did for a long time. I lived a half-life, on the edges of the world, thinking it just payment for the bargain we struck with the Fae, the bargain that saved our people. Then someone showed me otherwise and I found a way to break that curse. It can be the same for ye, brother. We will find a way to fix all this. All ye have to do is come home with me."

Logan held out his hand, his dark eyes boring into Cam. The moon shone down on the stones of Druach, illuminating the glade but outside the ring of standing stones the night was utterly dark. There was no sound. Even the sighing of the sea seemed to have fallen silent. Cam hesitated. Despite himself, he couldn't stop the flare of hope that ignited at Logan's words.

"This isnae a trick," Logan breathed. "Please, brother. Come home."

The voice was Logan's. The earnest, serious expression was Logan's. Cam found himself taking a step towards his brother, and then another. He reached out and clasped his brother's hand in the warrior's grip.

It was a mistake.

The moment his skin came into contact with Logan's, the rage of his curse roared up in him like an inferno. It came upon him so suddenly and so violently he had no time to prepare his defenses. With a strangled cry, his free will was swept away in a torrent of searing rage.

Cam looked at Logan and he no longer saw his elder brother. He no longer saw the man who'd taught him to ride or the man who'd interceded with their parents countless times when Cam had gotten himself into trouble. He didn't see the man who'd always had his back, who'd always been at his side when he needed him. Instead he saw the man who was the cause of all Cam's troubles. It was Logan who'd made the bargain with the Fae. It was Logan who'd dragged Camdan and Finlay into it. It was Logan's fault that Camdan had become a monster, bereft of everything he'd once held dear.

It was Logan's fault Cam had sent Beth away.

With a howl of animal rage, Cam grabbed Logan's sword and drew it, the sound shrill and unnatural in the still air. From somewhere nearby he thought he heard a woman's horrified scream but he ignored it. All that mattered was ending this man, the cause of all his problems. He swung their father's blade at Logan with all his strength, the metal glittering silver as it cut through the air.

Logan's expression didn't change. There was no fear on his face, only calm resignation. But as the blade swung for him he ducked under it, stepping neatly to the side and turning to face his brother, keeping Cam in full view and a distance of several meters between them.

"I willnae fight ye, brother," Logan said calmly. "Put down the sword."

Kill him! Kill him! raged the curse, surging through Cam's blood like liquid fire. His grip tightened on the sword hilt and he swung again, putting all his strength into a sideways slash that would have taken Logan's head off. Only Logan wasn't there anymore. Again, he danced nimbly away, lighter on his feet than a man of his size had any right to be. He met Cam's gaze and his eyes were shining with tears.

"Oh, my brother," he whispered. "What has been done to ye?"

This only made Cam angrier. His vision shifted and he no longer saw Logan. It was MacGregor standing in front of him, grinning widely.

"What are ye waiting for?" he said. "Ye want to kill me, dinna ye? Then do it. That's what ye are after all, isnae it? A mindless killer? That's what Beth thinks. Ye disgust her. Do ye know what she sees when she looks at ye? A monster. A rabid dog that needs to be put down. So why fight it? Be what ye are."

"I'll kill ye," Cam panted. "I'll kill ye."

But MacGregor just danced out of the way of his flashing blade, making no move to defend himself.

"Is that the best ye can do?" MacGregor hissed. "The mighty Camdan MacAuley, greatest warrior of Clan MacAuley. Ha! Ye are nothing more than a snivelling wretch!"

The vision shifted again and now it wasn't MacGregor standing before him, but a small, wizened old man with a hairless head and black eyes like pools of ink. Despite the rage of the curse, a sliver of fear slid through his stomach. He recognized this man. He wasn't a man at all but a Fae, the same creature he'd struck the bargain with all that time ago. The man grinned at him, eyes flashing with malevolence. In his hand he carried a branding iron. Its shape exactly matched the tattoo burned into Cam's forearm. Its tip glowed white-hot.

"Aye," the creature said, tilting his head as he regarded Cam with those dark eyes. "I'm most disappointed. Ye've turned out to be as weak as yer brothers and provide nay sport at all. Ye must fight, Camdan! Fight yer curse! The more ye wriggle, the tighter it becomes! Oh, such sweet torture!"

Camdan howled in rage. He sprang forward, swinging his father's sword in a series of lightning slashes that would have skewered any normal opponent. All reason evaporated. He must kill this creature. He must end it. Nothing else mattered. Nothing.

His tattoo flared hotter than it ever had, and the light that blared out from it was blinding. Dimly, some corner of his mind that still held onto sanity whispered a warning. This wasn't right. He was being tricked again. But the voice wasn't loud enough to drown out the rage that burned through him. His curse demanded release. It was time.

Time to let it destroy him.

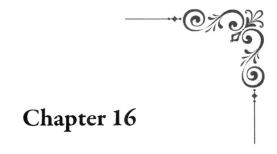

Chapter 16

Beside Beth, Thea screamed. "He's going to kill Logan!"
She clambered to her feet but then winced, one hand going to her swollen belly. She was pale and breathing heavily.

"Logan!" she breathed. "Holy shit, Beth. We have to stop this!"

Beth nodded. A cold, hard knot of fear had formed in her stomach, and it was all she could do to stop herself shaking. "You can't go running up there in your condition. Stay here."

"But I have to help Logan," Thea said fiercely.

"You have to stay here," Beth repeated, more firmly this time. "For your baby's sake."

Thea looked about to argue but then she nodded. She grabbed Beth's arm. "You have to stop them, Beth. Bring this madness to an end."

"I know," she replied with more confidence than she felt. "Trust me and stay here, right?"

Thea nodded. Beth turned to face the stone circle. Her stomach turned over. She was pretty sure Cam didn't see his brother anymore. His eyes were glazed, his lips curled in a snarl, the tattoo blazing on his arm so bright it lit the stone circle like a torch.

She had to stop this. If Cam killed his brother, he would never forgive himself. It would be the end of him.

She ran towards the stones, paying no heed to the mud that squished under her feet or the cold sea breeze that ripped at her hair.

But as she reached the circle, light suddenly flared and Beth was tossed through the air as though she was a piece of flotsam. She landed heavily on muddy grass, all the wind knocked out of her. Gulping in breaths, she flipped onto her stomach and looked around wildly. On the edges of her hearing, so faint she could almost believe she was imagining it, she thought she heard laughter.

"Fool!" A voice whispered on the sea breeze. "Do ye really think ye can defeat me? Paltry human! Ye have no power against the might of the Fae!"

A shiver went down Beth's spine. The voice dripped with malevolence and she felt as if cold, pitiless eyes were watching her. Anger welled up inside. Beth had always championed the little guy. The one who got trodden into the dirt by people and corporations more powerful than they were. This was what was happening here. The Fae creature with whom Cam had made his bargain had destroyed his life for no more reason than it could. Because it liked to watch him struggle, like a fly caught in a spider's web.

Fury pounded through Beth's veins. The injustice of it made her seethe. She struggled to her feet. "You think you've won?" she shouted into the wind. "You think it's that easy? Think again, buster!"

Pulling in a deep breath, Beth stalked across the damp ground to the edge of the circle. Squinting, she peered closer and made out a faint distortion in the air like heat haze. It shimmered between the stones, creating an invisible barrier.

Damn it! How the hell was she supposed to get through this? She thought furiously, dredging up everything she'd learned of the Fae.

They are of the mountains and the rivers, Cam had once told her. *Of the air and the sea. They hold power over the creatures and people of the Highlands and they will exercise that power however they see fit, regardless of the consequences.*

Beth paused. Power over the people of the Highlands? But she wasn't from the Highlands. She wasn't from Scotland at all. Hell, she wasn't even from this *time*.

Maybe that's why Irene came to the future, she thought. *Maybe only a person over whom the Fae hold no power could do what needs to be done.*

Irene herself had never used any sort of coercion on Beth. Instead, she had talked about choice and free will. *That's what it's always been about,* Beth thought as sudden understanding filled her. *Our choices. They are what shape us and determine our destiny.*

Lifting her chin and setting her jaw in determination, Beth took a step. "You have no power over me! I am from another land, another time, and I deny you!" She pulled her cell phone from her pocket. It was ruined now, just a lump of wires and plastic, but it was the only thing she still had from the twenty-first century. It was an anomaly that shouldn't be here. A piece of technology to negate the magic of the Fae.

Closing her eyes, Beth fixed her thoughts on her far distant homeland. She thought of TV commercials and video games. She thought of speeding cars and airplanes and taxis pelting along at crazy speeds. She thought of hospitals and medicines, and life-saving surgeries. She thought of all the things that made her anathema to the ancient magic of the Fae.

Then she took a step forward.

For a moment she felt something brush her skin, something like the stinging of wasps, but then the barrier vanished and Beth found herself stumbling into the ring of stones.

Ahead of her Cam and Logan were still locked in a deadly game of cat-and-mouse. Logan had a long gash down his left arm and he was obviously tiring. His movements as he dodged his brother's attacks were getting slower. Cam though, was still lightning fast, his movements almost a blur, his lips pulled back, showing his teeth in a snarl, and his eyes blazed with the same light that lit his tattoo.

Logan suddenly stumbled, losing his balance for a fraction of a second. Cam seized his chance. He leapt forward and brought the sword over his head in a two-handed grip, ready to deal a killing blow.

"No!" Beth screamed.

She sprinted across the clearing and threw herself between them. She grabbed Cam's sword-arm, trying desperately to hold it back. Her fingers closed around the blazing tattoo on his arm and it suddenly exploded into white light so dazzling that it blinded her.

When her vision cleared, she was no longer in the stone circle. She was standing in what looked to be the bar of an inn. A brawl was taking place. She recognized Cam in the middle of it, being set upon by four other men, all as big as he was. Cam laid about him with his fists, a manic grin on his face. One by one, he knocked out his opponents and then glared around at the rest of the room's occupants.

"Come on then!" he yelled. "Who's next!"

The patrons quickly shuffled away, fearful expressions on their faces. The madness faded from Cam's eyes and as reason asserted itself, Beth saw shame flare in his eyes.

The vision shifted and now she was riding with Cam at the head of a long column of men. MacGregor was riding by his side and he was counting gold coins and putting them in a pouch.

"A grand day, men!" he called, turning in his saddle to look at the outlaws riding behind him. "Thanks to our champion fighter here, we'll eat well tonight."

There was a ragged cheer and the men began chanting. Demon Blade! Demon Blade!

The scenes kept coming. Cam living alone in the wilds, eating only what he could hunt or trap. Sitting staring into the flames of a campfire, remembering everything he used to be. Taking work as a mercenary, fighting and killing for whoever would put food in his belly and give him a place to sleep.

She saw the man Cam thought he was.

No, she said to herself. *This isn't it. This isn't the sum of all he is. This isn't the man I fell in love with.*

Images tore at her, each one worse than the last. They came faster and thicker, deluging her with images that spoke of Cam's shame and self-loathing. It was difficult not to be swept away by them.

Damn it, she thought. *How am I supposed to stop this?*

Beth squeezed her eyes shut and concentrated, bringing to mind other images of Cam, memories of the time they'd spent together, memories of the man she saw when she looked at him. It was hard. Cam's thoughts battered at her, refusing to let her in, but she persevered, using the iron-willed stubbornness that every lawyer needed. Gritting her teeth, she forced her will over his. She opened her eyes and the image around her began to change.

This time she saw Cam crouching by young Travis, telling him a story whilst the boy laughed in delight. She saw him hauling logs with Rabbie as they built a goat pen on the Mac-Governs' lonely holding. She saw him spending hours scouring the hills, soaked to the skin as lightning cracked above, searching for one of Elspeth's lambs who'd gotten lost in foul weather. Beth saw Cam offer his aid to a strange woman in a clearing: Beth herself. She saw Cam take the necklace she'd given him to sell and tuck it carefully beneath his shirt and instead trade one of his own daggers so he could keep Beth's keepsake safe. She saw Cam pick himself up from where he'd laid unconscious on a mountain trail and, despite the pain of his wounded leg, begin to limp towards MacGregor's fortress, his face set in determination.

"You see?" she yelled into the maelstrom of images. "Do you understand now?"

There was movement behind her and Beth turned as a man approached her through the whirling images. It took a moment to recognize Cam. He looked younger, his expression less worn, more carefree. This must have been what he looked like before the curse took him, she realized. When he was still Camdan MacAuley, darling of the MacAuley clan.

He came to stand beside her. His blue eyes were clear, no longer full of shadow.

"Beth," he breathed. "I know what ye are trying to do. It's too late. I am what I am. The curse willnae allow me to escape."

"So that's it?" she snapped. "You're giving up? That's not the Camdan MacAuley I know! That man didn't flinch when faced by an angry mob baying for his blood—he stood and fought. Fight now, damn you!"

Something flashed in his eyes. Anger? Good. She needed him furious. A tiny vein throbbed in his temple and his jaw set. He looked around at the memories. Beth's memories. His eyes widened slightly.

"Aye," he breathed. "I had almost forgotten this man ye show me. Ye are right. The curse of the Fae made me a fighter. Now I'll show them just how fierce a fighter I can be." His jaw was set with determination and fire danced in his eyes.

He held out his hand and Beth took it. Together they turned and faced Cam's memories of himself. They were his demons—memories twisted by the magic of the Fae. But this time, instead of flinching, Cam's grip on Beth's hand tightened and he lifted his chin, straightened his shoulders, watching the memories play out in their entirety.

"Aye," he yelled. "I am that man. I did those things. But it isnae *all* I am. Do ye hear me? I willnae be yer puppet anymore! I accept the choices I made! And I will do better! Ye have nay power over me!"

For a moment the images whirled thicker and faster as though defying Cam's words but he stood resolute, watching each one with an unflinching gaze, acknowledging his past but no longer letting it dictate his future. And then, suddenly, the images burst into blinding white light and a blast of power exploded through the stones of Druach with enough force to send Beth flying through the air. She landed heavily on the ground, all the breath knocked out of her and everything went dark.

It took a moment for her to come to her senses. She blinked to clear her thoughts and then struggled up to sitting, pressing her hand to her head with a groan. Around her stretched the dark silence of the Highland night, punctuated only by the sounds of the sea. The moonlight showed that the stones of Druach had been knocked flat and now lay prone on the turf, great holes gouged into the earth where their bases had once stood. Cam and Logan were both coming around, blinking and looking as dazed as she was.

Cam scrubbed a hand across his face and looked around. "Beth? "he said. "Logan?" His tattoo had faded until it was all but invisible, just a faint tracery of shadow on his forearm. "It's...it's...gone. What does this mean?"

Beth found herself grinning. "What do you suppose it means, you great lummox? You did it! You broke your curse."

He shook his head. "Nay, lass. *We* did it."

Logan climbed unsteadily to his feet and looked around, his dark gaze taking in the fallen stones and then looking down at his brother. He held out his hand. Cam took it and Logan pulled him to his feet.

"I'm sorry, Logan," Cam began. "I didnae mean to—"

Logan cut off whatever he was about to say by pulling Cam into a bear-hug. There were tears shining in the big man's eyes. For a moment Cam went rigid, unsure how to respond, then he wrapped his arms around his brother and the two men embraced.

Beth scrambled to her feet. There were tears in her eyes too. Footsteps sounded and Thea pelted into the clearing, throwing herself at her husband who released Cam and put an arm around his wife's shoulders.

"You bloody idiot!" she cried. "Don't you ever do that to me again! I thought I was going to have a coronary back there!"

Logan smiled. "Cam, I would like ye to meet my wife, Thea. She, like yer Beth, is from another time and without her I wouldnae have been able to break my curse."

Cam gave an awkward bow. "An honor to meet ye, my lady." Then his eyes went to his brother. "It seems there's much to catch up on."

"Aye," Logan replied, clapping Cam on the shoulder. "I'll tell ye everything when we get home."

Cam went very still. "Home? Ye mean Dun Ringill?"

"Aye. Where else would I mean? It's past time that ye returned to yer family."

Cam nodded dumbly and Beth heard him whisper the word 'home' under his breath.

Logan glanced at Beth then back to Cam. He cleared his throat. "Come, my lady," he said to Thea. "We'll go and fetch the horses. The sooner we leave this accursed place the better."

The two of them quickly left the clearing, leaving Beth alone with Cam.

Neither spoke. Cam looked different: the slight stoop to his shoulders, like he constantly carried a heavy burden, was gone and his expression was less guarded, more open. Moonlight shone in his blue eyes as he regarded Beth in silence.

She wished she knew what he was thinking. She wished she knew whether he felt the same way she did. When Beth had battled his curse, when she'd forced him to see him how she saw him, all her feelings for him had been exposed. She'd held nothing back. Now he knew, unequivocally, how much she loved him. How much she needed him. She felt dangerously vulnerable. He held her heart in his hand and with one squeeze, he could crack it asunder.

Beth found herself breathing quickly. She wanted to say something, anything, to break the silence, but the words wouldn't come.

"Beth," he breathed, her name sounding like a promise as it filled the air between them.

She opened her mouth to speak. "Cam, I—"

She didn't get any further. Cam crossed the space between them so fast she barely registered the movement. He slammed into her, gathered her up, and wrapped her in his arms. His mouth came down on hers and suddenly he was kissing her fiercely, desperately. Heat roared to life along Beth's nerves and she found herself kissing him back, her arms circling his waist and pulling him hard against her. She lost herself in the sweet taste of him, his tongue dancing with her own, his hands pressed into the small of her back.

And suddenly she didn't need words. She didn't need Cam to tell her how he felt about her. He showed her instead. He showed her in the way he held her possessively. He showed her in the way his body trembled slightly under her touch. He showed her in the way he kissed her with a passion that took her breath away.

Eventually, he broke the kiss. A little breathless, Beth looked up at him. Cam cupped her face in his hands and gently pressed his forehead against hers. His eyes were silver pools of moonlight as he looked down at her.

"Ye saved me," he breathed.

Beth reached up and ran the tip of her finger down his stubbled jawline. "Ditto. I guess we're even then?"

He smiled, his fingers warm against her cheek. "Aye. Mayhap we are."

She breathed out slowly. "And now it's over. You can go home."

"I'm already home," he replied with a shake of his head. "I'm with ye. That's the only place I need to be." He placed a finger under her chin and tilted her head to look at him. "I love ye, lass. I dinna have the words to tell ye how much. Maybe my brother Finlay could come up with some fancy verse but I dinna have the skill. All I can tell ye is that I'm yers. All of me, for all time."

Beth's heart swelled. They were the words she'd been longing to hear and she thought she might burst from the sudden joy of it. Her lips pulled back and she smiled so hard her face hurt. God help her, she'd never known it was possible to feel like this. So...so...alive. So full of hope and promise.

"And I'm yours," she replied, the words catching in her throat. "I was since the very first moment I saw you. It just took me a while to realize it. I love you, Camdan MacAuley."

An answering grin, every bit as wide as Beth's, split Cam's face. His eyes sparkled, alight with joy. "Then stay with me," he said. "Stay with me for all time." He cleared his throat, took a deep breath and said, "Will ye marry me, Bethany Carter?"

The phrase exploded in her mind like a firework. Marry him? The ramifications shook her. Stay with him. Here, in sixteenth century Scotland and give up all thoughts of going home.

But I am home, she thought suddenly. *Wherever he is, I'm home.*

And then she had her answer.

"Of course I'll marry you," she whispered. "I thought you'd never ask."

With a whoop of joy Cam picked her up and spun her around until she yelled to be put down. Cam set her back on her feet and she staggered against him. He caught her, lowered his lips to hers and kissed her until her toes curled.

Chapter 17

"Oh my god," Thea said, examining herself sideways in the mirror. "Could I look any dumpier? I swear I've gotten fatter since this morning."

Beth glanced over at her friend. Thea was holding her breath and doing her best to stand up straight and tuck in her expanding stomach.

Beth laughed at Thea's comical expression. "You *are* having a baby you know? Getting bigger is kind of in the job description."

"That's no excuse to look like an overweight duck waddling about," Thea replied. She pointed an accusing finger at Beth. "I know bridesmaids aren't supposed to upstage the bride but this is ridiculous. This color shows every bulge! Why can't I wear black? At least that way people might not notice that I look like a tugboat!"

Beth shook her head and turned to Elspeth who was kneeling on the floor by Beth's feet, pinning up her train. "Help me out here, would you? Tell Thea she looks fine."

The red-haired woman looked up and raised an eyebrow. "I've tried. Three times I've explained that the cut of the dress is perfect for a pregnant woman and that the color highlights her eyes. Goes in one ear and out the other as my old ma used to say."

Thea planted her hands on her hips and then stuck her tongue out at them. Silence descended for a moment and then the three of them burst into laughter.

Beth was amazed and immensely pleased at how quickly the three of them had bonded. In the few short weeks since Beth and Cam moved into Dun Ringill and fetched Elspeth, Rabbie and Travis from the mountains, she, Thea and Elspeth had become firm friends. Both women showed a mischievous sense of humor and Thea had been indispensable in helping Beth adjust to life in the sixteenth century, having been through it herself when she came here over a year ago.

And wow, had there been a lot to get used to! Not least of all the fact that she now lived in a castle. A castle! Beth could hardly believe it. And it wasn't some drafty, cold damp castle either. Dun Ringill was beautiful. The halls and rooms were hung with tapestries, thick rugs covered the floors, and roaring fires blazed in the rooms, chasing away the Highland chill. It was always busy. Logan, along with members of his council, held court in the Great Hall, and there was a constant bustle of people coming and going and children getting under everyone's feet. After her somewhat solitary existence in the twenty-first century, Beth knew it would take some adjusting to but so far she loved it.

She wished her parents could see her now. They'd be so happy she'd found this life, even if it was a little unconventional. With a sigh, she pushed aside a little pang of sorrow. Her parents would be watching over her, she knew.

She climbed to her feet and, careful not to tread on the hem of her dress, crossed to the window. Outside stretched the wide courtyard of the inner bailey. It was busy. Logan's steward stood down there, overseeing the last minute preparations for the wedding. A cart had just rolled up laden with even more barrels of beer and the steward was supervising the unloading. The whole bailey was done out as though for a fair. There were games of skittles and hoopla set up, along with other things like tug of war and the caber toss.

Even the weather had decided to behave itself for her wedding day. The autumn storms of the last few days had blown through and now the sky was a vault of blue with wispy clouds like sheep scudding along above.

Yes, it had been a crazy few weeks but Beth wouldn't change them for the world. Cam, it had turned out, was incredibly popular within the clan and they'd been overjoyed to have him back. Gradually, bit by bit, he was assimilating back into clan life. He'd resumed his post as the garrison commander and now trained the clan's warriors every morning out on the tourney field. He'd taken a seat on Logan's council—along with Beth herself—and had already had several blazing rows with his brother—something, Beth was assured by the older members of the clan, which was perfectly normal. The only fly in the ointment was that they'd heard no word of the younger brother, Finlay and Beth knew this cut Camdan deeply.

After the wedding Logan and Cam were planning on leading an army into the mountains to route MacGregor and his cronies once and for all. Beth knew Cam was eager to ensure his old adversary faced the king's justice and eager to get Firefly back. But that worry could wait for another day.

A knock on the door startled Beth out of her reverie.

"That better not be you, Cam!" Thea shouted, waddling over to answer it. "It's the bride's prerogative to be a bit late!" But as she opened the door her voice trailed off and she gasped. "Beth," she called, her voice sounding a little uncertain. "There's somebody here to see you."

Beth turned and her heart skipped a beat as her eyes settled on her visitor.

Irene MacAskill.

The old woman looked exactly the same as when Beth saw her in Edinburgh all those miles, and all those years away. Same gray bun pinned to the back of her head, same cherub-like smile and rosy cheeks. She stepped into the room and stood with her hands clasped in front of her, smiling up at Beth.

Thea looked from Beth to Irene and back again. "Um, Elspeth, why don't we leave these two to talk?"

Elspeth, looking a little confused, took the hint. "Of course," she said, climbing to her feet. "We'll just be, um....outside."

She followed Thea out, shutting the door behind her. Beth was left alone with Irene.

The diminutive woman looked around curiously. "Well I must say I like what young Thea has done with the place," she said, nodding at the paintings on the wall and the dried flowers standing in vases around the room. "I always said this place needed a woman's touch. She's fitted into her role as mistress of the castle as though she was born for it. Which, of course, she was."

"What do you want, Irene?" Beth asked, unable to keep the heat from her voice. The woman chose to turn up *now*? On her wedding day? After throwing her back in time and then abandoning her?

"What do I want?" Irene replied. "What I always want: to see the balance restored."

"And what the hell is that supposed to mean?"

Irene smiled and walked right up to Beth. She was so short she barely reached Beth's chin and stood gazing up at her with her midnight eyes. "Ye look well, dear. Yer skin is fairly glowing! It seems my homeland agrees with ye."

Beth resisted the urge to back away. "Have you come to whisk me away again? To throw me through time without so much as a by-your-leave?"

Irene's smile didn't falter. "Only if ye wish me to."

"Damn you, Irene!" Beth exploded. "This isn't a game! This is my *life* you're talking about! What right did you have to meddle with it without my permission? What right did you have to send me back here?"

Irene cocked her head. "Would ye rather I hadnae?"

Beth opened her mouth and closed it again. If Irene hadn't sent her back here, she wouldn't have met Cam and that thought was unthinkable. "Well, no," she managed at last. "But you could have asked me first."

"I'm nay sure I understand ye, my dear. Are ye saying ye were forced to come here? That isnae what happened at all. If ye remember, I explained that ye would be going to an unknown place and that yer road would be a difficult one. The choice was yers to make, as it always must be. Ye made that choice, not I." She smiled up at Beth like a kindly old grandmother.

Beth's anger drained away. Irene was right. She might not have known exactly what she was getting into when she stepped through that archway but she'd been willing to take the risk. She'd been willing to walk into the unknown in search of the thing she'd always been searching for.

"And did ye find it, my dear?" Irene asked as if reading her thoughts.

"I did," Beth breathed. "I found more than I could have ever imagined."

Irene patted her arm. "I'm glad. It was a difficult path ye had to walk, my dear, more difficult than most, but I knew ye had the courage needed. Ye made the right choice. Now ye must make another."

Beth looked at her sharply. "What do you mean?"

"I've come to give ye a second choice. If ye wish it, I will send ye home, back to yer own time."

A slight gasp escaped Beth. Home? She could go home? When she'd first arrived in this time going home was all she'd wanted. If Irene had turned up during those first few days, Beth would have accepted her offer in a heartbeat. But now? Now things were very, very different.

"I *am* home," she replied. "It took me a while to realize that. There's nothing for me in the twenty-first century. Everything I need is here: family. Friends. The love of my life. Why would I want to leave?"

Irene's grin broadened. "Ah! Spoken like a true child of the Highlands! And here's me thinking all ye ever wanted in life was that internship, eh?"

Beth smiled wryly. "I thought that too. I was wrong. Since my parents died all I thought about was becoming a lawyer: that it would somehow help me put the world to rights. But I don't need to be in the twenty-first century to do that. There are so many people here I can help."

She'd already been given a seat on Logan's council to advise him on all sorts of legal matters. Young Travis was training as her aide, a role which the boy had taken to whole-heartedly, and already Beth had all sorts of ideas on how to improve the justice system and help those who needed it.

It was ironic, she thought, that after her utter abhorrence of violence, she was about to marry a warrior. But she'd learned that things were never as simple as she thought. There weren't good people and bad people, just varying shades of gray.

"Aye, lass," Irene replied. "Ye will live a fine life here and other lives will be better off for having ye in them. I'm happy for ye, my dear." She patted Beth's cheek and turned away.

Beth touched her shoulder. "Wait. I never said thank you."

"Nay need, my dear," Irene replied with a smile. "The balance is restored. That is thanks enough for me."

"Will I ever see you again?"

The old woman shrugged. "Who knows? Even I canna see every future. Mayhap our paths will cross again someday. Until then, have a grand life, Bethany Carter."

With that the old woman walked to the door and left. A moment later Elspeth's head poked around the door and the red-haired woman hurried to Beth's side.

"Are ye all right?" she asked. "Thea told me who that was. A Fae! Right here in the castle! I can hardly credit it!"

"I'm fine," Beth replied. "Irene just came to wish me well for the wedding. Where's Thea?"

"Talking to Irene. Seems she and Thea are old friends too. Whist! Does everyone in this castle know a friendly Fae?"

Beth laughed. "No, only the foolish ones. And believe me, most of the Fae are *not* friendly."

The door opened and Thea came in, her hand on her swollen belly. She looked decidedly uncertain.

"Are you okay?" Beth asked.

Thea nodded. "I...think so. I asked if Irene would come and help me with the birth and she gave me quite a shock. She reckons I'm having twins!"

"That's wonderful!" Elspeth cried, hugging Thea tight. "Then today is a double celebration!"

"All the same," Thea said with a sheepish grin. "I think it might be best to wait until after the wedding to tell Logan. When he finds out he's having *two* sons he might very well have twins of his own!"

They all burst out laughing. From outside came the sound of a bell ringing.

"Midday!" Beth cried. "We're late!"

In a hurry, she took one last look in the mirror, pushed a few strands of hair from her face, brushed down the beautiful red and gold wedding gown that the castle seamstresses had made for her, and then with Thea and Elspeth on either side, Beth swept from the room.

The corridors that led to the Great Hall were strewn with late-blooming flowers and a delicious scent filled the air as they walked. Nerves began to wriggle in Beth's belly and her heart began to pound. Oh God, she was getting married! She could still hardly believe it.

They reached the door to the Great Hall and paused. The door stood open and through it Beth saw rows of people crammed into the space, all looking at her expectantly. A piper began to play and, accompanied by its song, the three women swept into the hall. Beth's eyes sprang to the far end of the room, searching for Cam. There. He stood by the high table, dressed in the traditional MacAuley plaid over a crisp white linen shirt. His copper and gold hair fell onto his shoulders in soft waves and a ceremonial sword glittered at his side. Rabbie, freshly shaved and looking neater than Beth had ever seen him, stood by Cam's side and Logan faced the two of them, his hands clasped as he waited.

Beth's heart skipped a beat at the sight of her intended. He was so god-damned handsome. So god-damned...everything. Cam's winter-blue eyes found hers across the distance. Beth began walking down the aisle but barely noticed the people turn to watch her. All her attention was fixed on the man she loved.

He watched her intently, hardly blinking as she moved down the aisle to stand by his side. Only when she reached him did he break into a wide, boyish smile that made his eyes sparkle.

"Lord, Beth," he breathed. "Ye are a sight to set a man's blood pounding."

"You don't scrub up too bad yourself," she murmured.

Cam took her hands and together they turned to face Logan. The laird of the MacAuley looked resplendent in his ceremonial plaid and his velvet cloak of office. He didn't smile as he looked them over but his eyes twinkled with merriment.

"One of the most rewarding duties a laird can perform is the marriage of two of his people. Today is such a day, made even more special because today it is the wedding of my brother, Camdan MacAuley, to Lady Bethany Carter. I thought this day might never come and it gladdens my heart to stand here and welcome them both into Clan MacAuley."

A round of cheering filled the hall. Beth glanced at the guests and saw row upon row of smiling faces, the faces of her new clan, her new family. Her heart constricted and Cam squeezed her hand reassuringly.

Cam spoke his vows first, his hands gripping hers tightly as he gazed down at her, making promises that would bind him to her for the rest of their lives. Then it was Beth's turn. The words rolled off her tongue as easily as if they'd been lining up.

And then it was done.

With one of his rare smiles, Logan pronounced them husband and wife and, to cheers from the guests, Cam swept her into his arms and kissed her long and hard.

THE FEAST THAT FOLLOWED was louder, busier and brasher than any wedding Beth had ever attended. There was eating, drinking, dancing and games. Clan MacAuley sure knew how to party. Ale, wine and whisky flowed all afternoon and long into the evening and she lost count of the number of delicious dishes that were brought out of the kitchen by an army of serving staff.

Night had fallen and candlelight lit the Great Hall. Beth leaned back in her chair and took another sip of wine. How much had she drunk? Certainly enough to be a little tipsy.

The center of the Great Hall had been kept clear for dancing and Beth had taken part in so many that her feet were aching. She'd begged off the next dance and went to slump in her chair, leaving Cam down there with the musicians. He and

Travis had joined in playing with the quartet, Travis on the flute, Cam on the lute, and now a jaunty tune filled the Great Hall, with many of the guests clapping along.

Beth watched Cam as he played and smiled to herself. The tune finished and Cam struck up another, leading the hall in singing what sounded to Beth like an extremely rude drinking song. Elspeth hurried down from her seat to cover young Travis's ears and everyone laughed.

Cam looked up and their eyes met across the Hall. His smile widened and Beth raised her wine glass in toast to her new husband.

Cam finished the song and handed the lute back to the musicians. He crossed the hall, weaving through the people who were forming up for the next dance, and came to her side. His cheeks were flushed, his red-gold hair shining in the candle-light.

"How about we get out of here?" he asked, his voice low and breathless.

She grinned at him. "I thought you'd never ask."

Cam bent, grabbed her round the waist, and suddenly threw her over his shoulder. A chorus of cheering erupted as he carried her to the stairs and Beth felt her cheeks burning. Yet she didn't protest as her husband carried her up the stairs and into their chamber. Only when he'd shut the door behind them did he set her on her feet again.

Beth looked up at him. He was peering around the chamber, an odd look on his face.

"What is it?"

"I was just...remembering," he said softly. "This was my chamber when I was a boy. There are so many memories and now here we are, about to create a whole host of new ones together. Sometimes I think I'm dreaming. Sometimes I think this isnae real."

Beth took his hand and gently placed it over her heart. "Feel that? It's real."

Cam flattened his palm against her chest and then took her hand and placed it over his own heart. "I love ye, Beth. I love ye so hard and so deep sometimes I can barely breathe."

She could feel his heartbeat under her hand. It was pounding and she realized that Cam was every bit as terrified and exhilarated as she. She moved his hand lower to cup her breast and a low hiss escaped his lips. His pupils were huge, turning his eyes dark, and in them Beth saw raw, naked desire.

He stepped close, putting an arm around her waist and jerking her hard against him. He bent his head and his mouth covered hers, his kiss deep and urgent. Arousal flared to life in Beth's veins and she found herself tugging at Cam's clothes. She wanted him. All of him. Now.

Cam obliged her by tearing off his plaid and stepping out of it and then pressing the length of his naked body against hers so she felt the contour of every muscle through the thin material of her dress and the hardness of the bulge digging into her stomach. He kissed her fiercely, his mouth caressing hers whilst his hands moved behind her back and deftly untied the laces of her dress. The garment fell to the ground and suddenly there was nothing between them but skin and heat.

Cam's hands trailed down her back to her buttocks whilst Beth wrapped her arms around his neck. With a low moan Cam put his hands under her backside and lifted her and Beth wrapped her legs around his waist. The tip of his manhood bumped against her, sending a hot spear of need right through her body.

Cam carried her to the bed and laid her gently on the covers. He knelt over her, his eyes taking in every inch of her bare skin as though committing it to memory.

"My love," he breathed. "I must have ye."

"Then what are you waiting for?" Beth gasped.

He nudged her knees apart and lowered himself on top of her. Beth raised her legs and wrapped them around his waist, inviting him in. He gave her what she wanted. With a hard, deep thrust, Cam pierced her core, driving himself all the way in.

Beth cried out, bucking against him as a hot wave of sensation deluged her. Cam thrust in again and Beth ground her hips against his, her fingers digging into the hard muscles of his back as scalding waves of sensation rocked her body. Cam's tempo increased and he plunged hard into her, claiming her. The headboard slammed against the wall and cries of pleasure were torn from Beth's throat as she felt her man filling her, answering a deep, desperate need.

It was too much. With a shudder Beth came apart, all her thoughts exploding in a blinding conflagration of ecstasy that tore through her. She arched beneath him, her nails gouging into his flesh, and screamed his name at the ceiling.

Cam went rigid and then growled deep in his throat as he thrust one last time, spilling himself deep within her. He held himself motionless for a few heartbeats and collapsed atop her, his delicious weight pinning her to the bed, his hoarse breathing loud by her ear. For one long, timeless moment, Beth remained still, breathing in his scent.

Then Cam raised himself onto his hands and gazed down at her. Their gazes met, neither speaking. No words were needed. Slowly, he leaned down and kissed the tip of her nose before rolling onto his back and pulling her against him. Beth rolled onto her side and slotted her body alongside his. His arm cradled her possessively and she rested her head on his muscled chest, listening to the wild thump of his heart.

It was done. They were joined, and always would be.

My husband, she thought as she lazily ran her fingers along the contours of Cam's chest. *My home. My future.*

Tomorrow her new life would begin. Tomorrow. For tonight there was just herself and the man she loved and their wedding night stretching ahead. Beth intended to make the most of it.

She raised herself onto her elbow and cocked her head at him. "Okay. Round one wasn't bad. Let's see if we can make round two even better."

He grinned at her. "Round two is it? There will be many more rounds than that if I have my way." With a growl he grabbed her and kissed her and all rational thought went right out of Beth's head.

Oh, yes. The night had only just begun.

THE END

WANT SOME MORE HIGHLAND adventure? Then why not try the other books in the series? www.katybaker-books.com

Would you like to know more of Irene MacAskill's story? *Guardian of a Highlander,* a free short story is available as a free gift to all my newsletter subscribers. Sign up below to grab your copy and receive a fortnightly email containing news, chat and more. www.katybakerbooks.com

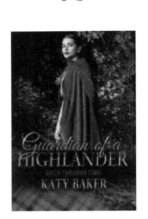

WHAT DO YOU DO WHEN destiny comes knocking?

Irene Buchanan is running from hers. Gifted with fae blood, she is fated to become the Guardian of the Highlands.

But Irene wants none of it. Soon to be married to her childhood sweetheart, she has everything she ever dreamed of. Why would she risk that for a bargain with the fae?

But Irene can't run forever. When a terrifying act of violence rips all she loves from her, she realizes she must confront her destiny. If she doesn't, she risks the destruction of all she holds dear.

The fate of the Highlands lies in her hands.

Printed in Great Britain
by Amazon